"Lying down on the job, I see," Rafe said, his smile widening as he noticed the bits of grass clinging to Jeannie's blouse.

She dropped her horse's reins and raised her palms in a gesture of surrender. "Caught red-handed."

"Wet-handed is more like it." Rafe dismounted and let his horse drink from the clear-running creek. Jeannie could feel the swift pace of the blood in her veins as he approached her.

"I got so thirsty looking for stray calves, I decided to stop and get a drink," she told him softly.

"Did you get any?" he asked, a lazily seductive gleam in his eyes as he plucked a blade of grass from her collarbone.

"Not a one." Her voice slipped a notch when he lifted a piece of green from the tail of the shirt knotted over her stomach.

"Too bad," he murmured. His thumb moved up to the deep vee of her neckline to whisk away a blade stuck to her first button. Slowly but thoroughly, Rafe picked her shirt clean, the light touch of his hands filling her with unspoken desire.

They hadn't been alone all day, they'd been with all the cowboys out for the branding. Now it was just Rafe and Jeannie, one man and one woman.

"Come here," he said gruffly, and she gladly obeyed his command.

It was no gentle embrace they shared. He caught her corn-silk hair in one hand, clamped the other on the bare skin between her shirt and jeans, and pulled her against him. She dug her nails into the muscles of his back, and arched into him. . . .

WHAT ARE *LOVESWEPT* ROMANCES?

They are stories of true romance and touching emotion. We believe those two very important ingredients are constants in our highly sensual and very believable stories in the *LOVESWEPT* line. Our goal is to give you, the reader, stories of consistently high quality that may sometimes make you laugh, sometimes make you cry, but are always fresh and creative and contain many delightful surprises within their pages.

Most romance fans read an enormous number of books. Those they truly love, they keep. Others may be traded with friends and soon forgotten. We hope that each *LOVESWEPT* romance will be a treasure—a "keeper." We will always try to publish

LOVE STORIES YOU'LL NEVER FORGET
BY AUTHORS YOU'LL ALWAYS REMEMBER

The Editors

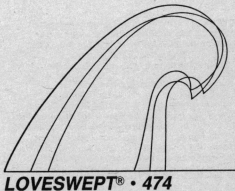

LOVESWEPT® • 474

Fran Baker
San Antonio Rose

BANTAM BOOKS
NEW YORK • TORONTO • LONDON • SYDNEY • AUCKLAND

SAN ANTONIO ROSE

A Bantam Book / June 1991

If you would be interested in receiving protective vinyl
covers for your Loveswept books, please write to this address
for information:

Loveswept
Bantam Books
P.O. Box 985
Hicksville, NY 11802

ISBN 0-553-44119-1

Published simultaneously in the United States and Canada

PRINTED IN THE UNITED STATES OF AMERICA

OPM   0 9 8 7 6 5 4 3 2 1

Prologue

A car was coming, judging by that cloud of dust down the road, and the restless girl watching from her second-story bedroom window could hardly wait to see who was driving it.

It wasn't bad enough that she could see her mother's grave, with a single yellow rose marking the spot, from the window. Or that her father had buried himself under a mountain of paperwork in his first-floor office. But even the ranch manager, who doted on her as if she were his own flesh and blood, had packed up his saddlebags the morning after the funeral and ridden off into the hills to mourn alone.

Callers of any stripe, then, were a welcome

sight as far as the twelve-year-old girl was concerned.

With a toss of her head, she flipped her twin blond braids over her narrow shoulders. Then she crossed her arms on the windowsill and kept her eyes peeled for the vehicle that was creating that dirty cumulus in its wake.

She didn't have long to wait. No sooner had she settled herself, in fact, than a badly dented maroon Studebaker with two blue doors on the driver's side turned onto the gravel lane leading to the ranch yard. The old car bounced and belched smoke something terrible before it finally came to a stop in front of the house.

When a man in a battered straw hat, baggy work clothes, and sandals made from tires got out, followed by a boy wearing a bright red bandanna, she realized they were probably migrant workers looking for a job. Crowded into the backseat were a woman and two other youngsters, hope warring feebly with the expectation of another rebuff on the faces they pressed to the window.

Trying to beat the doorbell, the girl went tearing out her bedroom and down the stairs. She yanked open the front door, startling the man who was standing there. At the same time her father, who'd probably seen the Studebaker from his office window, came out.

No one moved or spoke for several seconds

as the cattle rancher glared impatiently at the two callers. A fifth-generation Texan who'd been wet-nursed on the atrocities at the Alamo, the rancher had no earthly use for Santa Ana's descendants. Worse yet, he was a recent widower with no sons to carry on his name and a daughter to raise. A daughter who, with her golden hair, gray eyes, and baby-powder skin, was the spitting image of his late wife.

"Speak your piece and speak it in English," he commanded gruffly. "And then get the hell off my land."

The boy stiffened as if he'd just been struck. He was older than the girl by four years or so, and several inches taller. He wore denim jeans and a clay-red shirt, both faded by numerous washings. His hair was as black and shiny as a crow's wing. His skin had the coppery hue of his Spanish ancestors, his straight nose and high cheekbones the noble structure. But it was his eyes that fascinated her, for they were the most beautiful shade of midnight blue she'd ever seen.

Suddenly aware that the boy was examining her as closely as she was him, the girl blushed and dropped her gaze to the scuffed toes of his tennis shoes. But her heart took wing and her stomach went weightless, and she felt forever changed by their moment of mutual curiosity.

Three days later the Mexican moved his wife

and children into the largest unit of the furnished fourplex that housed the help. Six years and two broken hearts after that, the entire family just up and disappeared in the middle of the night. . . .

One

Half the people gathered in the family cemetery had come to pay their last respects to a true son of Texas. The other half had come to make damn sure that Big Tom Crane was dead.

Rafe Martinez parked his '63 Corvette Stingray in the only available space in the ranch yard, between a Ford F-150 pickup brandishing a gunrack in the back window and a flashy pink Cadillac flaunting a pair of longhorns on the front grille. He thought about gunning the motor—just once, for old time's sake—then thought again and switched off the ignition.

Eleven years in exile had transformed him, but it certainly hadn't tamed him. The thick black hair skimming his white shirt collar was still too long by any cattleman's standards; the matte-metal shades resting on his cheekbones raised more than one eyebrow; and that small silver stud glittering in the lobe of his left ear was a real shocker.

Those remnants of rebellion aside, Rafe had a style all his own. In the land of Stetsons and Western-styled suits, he went bareheaded and wore European-cut clothes that emphasized his broad shoulders, trim waist, and long runner's legs. A hand-painted silk tie replaced its traditional string counterpart; woven ramie suspenders took the place of a gaudy gold or silver belt buckle. The expensive watch on his wrist told him the time and told everyone else he'd arrived.

His single concession to Lone Star fashion was a pair of hand-stitched black lizard boots. Not only did the soft leather pamper his long, narrow feet, but the extra two inches the heels added to his lean six-foot frame would give him a better view of the gringos' bald spots when they respectfully removed their hats.

Rafe took off his sunglasses and put them in his breast pocket, then got out of his car and joined the solemn procession across the gravel lane to the grave. He walked with confidence, each movement flowing naturally into the next, as befitted both a successful attorney and a rising star on the political scene.

A state senator, famous for courting the

Hispanic vote and then promptly forgetting his promises, went out of his way to shake Rafe's hand. More jobs for minority contractors on the Alamo Sportsdome, the Anglo legislator pledged with sweaty-palmed desperation. And an appointment to the aquifer task force for the person of Rafe's choosing.

It was a classic case of too little too late. His countenance as hard and full of mystery as the face of an Aztec lord, Rafe extricated his hand. He silently renewed his vow to see the senator defeated in next year's primary.

But primary day was a long way off, and he had business to tend to now. Sun dapple and shadows enveloped him when he passed through the open, ornate gates that cordoned off the cemetery where Big Tom would be laid to rest beside his long-deceased wife, Laurrinda.

If nothing else, Rafe thought as he crossed the soft carpet of spring grass, it was a flawless day for a funeral.

The Hill Country had shed its January dullness and draped itself in April's brilliance. Live oaks and pecan trees sported tender green leaves. The birds wore their brightest plumage. Bluebonnets and Blackfoot daisies blanketed the broad-topped hills as far as the eye could see.

The ranch house, a Victorian monstrosity within sight of the family cemetery, resurrected memories of a sweeter spring when virile juices had pumped through Rafe's body and young love had blossomed in his heart. The bitter winters that followed had seared his pride and scarred his soul. They had also strengthened his resolve to prove himself. And prove himself he had. Beyond anyone's wildest dreams, his own included.

Rafe had left his San Antonio law office at nine that morning and driven the forty miles northeast with the Corvette's windows open and its powerful engine purring like a cat with a bellyful of cream. He reached his highway exit in record time. Or maybe it only seemed that way because he was running on gasoline these days instead of his glands.

The road he took then—originally a bison path, later an offshoot of the thousand-mile *camino real*—had been paved at some point since his departure. No matter. He knew its curves as intimately as he'd known those of the girl who used to wait for him at trail's end.

Like Rafe, the state of Texas had undergone tremendous change in recent years. Crude-oil prices had dropped to a depressing low in the unlamented eighties. As had consumer demand for well-marbled steaks. On the bright side, at least to his way of thinking, language barriers had diminished. And Hispanics had demolished long-standing hurdles in San Antonio politics by taking intermittent control of city hall and the county courthouse.

Only the Circle C had remained unchanged,

he realized immediately upon his arrival. Except for the necessary improvements, the sprawling ranch looked virtually the same as when he'd left it—a wire-fenced stronghold that had weathered everything from Comanche Indian attacks to a crippling downturn in the economy.

It remained to be seen how well it would weather Rafe's return.

Noticing that the mourners had formed a wide arc around the grave, he deliberately but politely worked his way to the front.

A municipal court judge whose ruling he'd appealed just last week nodded silently to him. Cattle ranchers who'd bent many an elbow with Big Tom eyed him suspiciously, while cowhands who'd ridden for the brand with Rafe tipped the brims of their hats in a welcome-back salute. The barons' diamond-bedecked wives gaped at him in stunned surprise; their designer-dressed daughters gave him the once over . . . twice.

Rafe's face was as smooth and cool as the marble desktop in his office, and he let no one and nothing deter him as he took his place and assumed the traditional pose of funereal respect—feet spraddled about six inches apart, and the palm of one hand clasping the back of the other over his lower abdomen.

He wanted to see the woman who stood on the opposite side of the polished bronze casket. And he wanted her to see him.

Jeannie . . . He almost said her name aloud when he spotted her clinging to the arm of the longtime ranch manager, Rusty Pride. Beside her stood a dark-haired boy of about ten who looked vaguely familiar, behind her a man whom he didn't recognize but who hovered over her with husbandly concern.

The old hurt rushed back, sharpened on the whetstone of that long-ago betrayal.

Rafe tried to staunch the flow of memories, to forget the past and focus on the present. But they'd merged before his very eyes, in the vision of elegance standing little more than an arm's length away.

A faille-trimmed, floppy-brimmed black straw hat covered Jeannie's head, but Rafe remembered how her hair caught sunbeams and threw them shining back to the sky. Angel hair, he'd called it then.

The shaped jacket and slim skirt of her silk suit showcased a figure that had more than fulfilled its womanly promise. Pearl earrings shone discreetly at the juncture of her delicate jawline and gracefully arched neck. A faint iridescence shimmered from the sheer black stockings sheathing her slender legs. The leather pumps that shod her feet completed the portrait of feminine perfection.

She turned to run a comforting hand over the boy's hair, smoothing down a cowlick in the process, and Rafe got a glimpse of her face beneath her swooping hat brim. A beautiful face, even in grief. She turned still more, absently scanning the half-moon of mourners on the other side of the grave, and their gazes met and held.

A moment of shocked awareness sizzled between them.

"Let us pray," the minister said, opening his black psalter to begin the simple Protestant service.

Everyone bowed their heads . . . except Rafe and Jeannie.

The minister's monotone drifted above the silent gathering as the blue-eyed boy from the barrio and the golden-haired girl from Bolero stared at each other across the flower-covered coffin.

How was it possible that, even in death, her father could keep them apart?

For a fraction of a moment, Jeannie Crane thought her eyes were playing tricks on her.

It wouldn't be the first time she'd mistaken a tall, dark-haired man for Rafe Martinez. Every once in a while she would spot someone whose muscular build or macho bearing reminded her of him. Her heart would lodge in her throat until she realized she was staring at a stranger. Then she would turn away, relief and regret fighting for the upper hand on her emotions.

But there was no mistaking those blue eyes

that still haunted her while asleep and awake. No confusing that proud nose and those prominent cheekbones with someone else's. And absolutely no doubt about the crisply etched mouth that had so beguiled her at eighteen.

The memories were eleven years old but the pain was as fresh as if it all had happened yesterday.

"Are you all right?" Rusty whispered.

Jeannie tore her gaze away from Rafe and looked at the loyal ranch manager. He wore a brown suit that was nearly as old as he, and, beneath the brim of his black Stetson, an expression that was partly puzzled and partly pained. She glanced down then, and seeing that she had his arm in a death grip, apologetically relaxed her hold.

"Yes," she answered softly. "I'm fine."

The minister droned on. A bee buzzed lazily around the wreath of yellow roses lying atop Big Tom's coffin. The breeze spanked a streamer from the white satin bow that bound the flowers to the lid. And those blue eyes drew her gaze from across the way like a magnet that defied resistance.

By sheer force of will Jeannie shut it all out and bowed her head. Try though she might, she couldn't stave off the thought that history was repeating itself. That once again she was torn between Big Tom and Rafe Martinez.

Everyone had called her father Big Tom,

including Jeannie. Part of it was conditioning—she'd never heard him called anything else. And part of it was his comportment—standing six-five in his stocking feet and weighing in at two hundred fifty pounds in his prime, he'd ruled his widespread cattle kingdom with the proverbial iron hand.

But all the king's money and all the king's men hadn't kept his princess of a daughter from falling in love with the son of a peon.

"Ashes to ashes . . ." the minister intoned.

One of the six cowhands serving as pall-bearers removed the bouquet of roses and set it aside before rejoining the others. Together they lowered their late boss's coffin into the grave.

"Dust to dust . . ."

Rusty gently disengaged Jeannie's hand from his arm and stepped forward to shovel a spadeful of the rich Texas earth onto the lid. The dirt landed with a *clump* that essentially brought the simple service to an end.

She rested her hand on her son's heaving shoulder and rubbed it gently. Then fighting tears of her own, she joined in the final "Amen."

"Miss Jeannie Crane has asked me to thank all of you for your attendance today and to invite you to the house for refreshments," the minister said as he closed his prayer book.

The mourners began converging on her before filing out of the cemetery. Hands squeezed hers. Murmured condolences came from all sides. Somehow she managed to respond, returning clasps and consolations in grateful fashion.

Rafe didn't cross over with the others, but it seemed each time she turned to visit with another guest, he managed to be in her line of vision. Because of their proximity, and because they were acquainted with so many of the same people, Jeannie had known this day would eventually come. But now that the moment of truth had arrived, she found herself totally unprepared for it.

She developed a slight backache from standing so rigidly, and the beginnings of a headache from the tension. Only the thought that she was the one who'd been left in the lurch got her through the endless formalities without falling apart.

Rusty stood devotedly at her side, shaking hands and directing traffic. When the throng thinned out, he looked over at the lone man standing tall against the Texas sky and demanded, "What's *he* doing here?"

Jeannie followed the course of Rusty's glare, her mouth going dry and her palms becoming damp. But before she could form a reply, a gentle hand gripped her elbow and turned her around. Grateful for this small reprieve, she lifted her gaze to Webb Bishop's intelligent face.

Webb had been Big Tom's cardiologist and

Jeannie's shoulder to cry on these past eighteen months. Divorced for several years, he was one of the kindest, most considerate men she'd ever met. And lately she'd gotten the impression that he was interested in expanding their relationship from the professional to the personal.

She felt a twinge of guilt as she looked up into his brown eyes, which shone with a patience that had never worn thin. The problem was—

"Are you ready to go back to the house?" he asked her now.

She shook her head. "Not quite."

"I'm hungry," Tony complained, his grief taking a temporary backseat to his growling stomach.

Every protective instinct Jeannie possessed came into play as she turned back to her son. Her heart knocked out a warning at the sight of his tear-streaked face, so like the one she'd loved and lost.

For all his failings as a father, Big Tom had been an exemplary grandfather. Maybe he'd seen Tony as the son he never had. Or maybe he'd finally seen the error of his prejudiced ways. Whatever, the gruff cattle rancher had taken one look at the baby boy in the crib beside his daughter's hospital bed and fallen hopelessly in love.

"Why don't you walk back to the house with Rusty and Webb?" Her voice sounded remarkably calm considering she felt as if she was on the verge of a breakdown. "I'll be along shortly."

"Say the word, and I'll stay," Rusty assured her.

Time had drawn craggy lines in his face and faded the red hair, which accounted for his nickname, to the color of fine silver. There was a permanent squint to his eyes from long years of riding into the sun and the wind. Bucking broncos and stampeding cattle had broken almost every bone in his body.

But his age and infirmities aside, Rusty could still outrope, outride, and outfight many a younger man. He was the last cowboy, gallant to the core where ladies were concerned. And just as he would have done anything at one time to protect her mother, so Jeannie knew he would have laid down his life for her and for Tony right now.

She smiled at his offer to stay but shook her head in refusal. "I'd rather you keep an eye on things at the house."

"Well, to tell you the truth," he said, "I was planning to go back to my place and change clothes."

As foreman, Rusty lived in a small bungalow instead of the fourplex the other unmarried cowhands called home. It was about a mile from the main house, and it wasn't fancy by any stretch of the imagination. But it was one of the privileges of rank. And it guaranteed him some privacy after a day spent moving cattle and bossing men.

He gave the brim of his Stetson a tug and her a shrug. "I figured I'd ride out and finish getting a calf count so you can order the supplies we'll need for branding next week."

That gave Jeannie an idea. "Maybe Tony could go with you."

"All right!" came Tony's jubilant cry.

"I thought you were hungry," Rusty said with a teasing smile.

"I'll eat fast," Tony promised.

"Not *too* fast," Jeannie insisted.

"Awww, Mom."

"Have Martha feed him at the kitchen table," Jeannie instructed the ranch manager. The words *just in case* remained unspoken, but they shimmered in the air between them.

Rusty nodded as if to say he'd gotten the rest of her message, then reached over to ruffle Tony's thick hair with a gnarled hand. "C'mon, cowpoke, let's go see what that crotchety old cook has rustled up."

"I hope she made tacos," Tony said as he fell into step beside the foreman. At nine going on ten he was tall for his age, his dark head already coming to Rusty's shoulder. "They're my favorite."

Webb's gaze swung to Rafe, then back to Jeannie's pale, drawn face. She'd told him the whole shameful story of course. How could she not? Now she could practically see him making the connection in his mind.

"I'll wait here with you," he said staunchly.

"Please, Webb . . ." She laid her hand on his arm, pleading for his understanding. "I have to do this alone." When still he hesitated, she hastened to add, "Maybe I can keep him away from the house."

The logic of her argument must have finally convinced him. He looked at Rafe one last time, then dropped a dry peck on her smooth, porcelain cheek before rounding on his heel and hurrying to catch up with Rusty and Tony.

Jeannie waited until she was sure the three of them were out of earshot before she turned, head spinning and heart slamming against the walls of her chest, to face the father of her son.

Two _____

Rafe started toward her, skirting the gaping hole in the ground with long, fluid strides.

Jeannie stood perfectly still, but the slight quiver to her lower lip betrayed her anxiety over the confrontation that had been such a long time coming.

Through the years she had fantasized about seeing him again. She had pictured herself bumping into him by accident on the crowded streets of San Antonio or in the close confines of a dinner party. They would make polite conversation, never referring to the past, and she would take her secret with her when she took her leave.

But his reputation preceded him now. He was a highly paid, hard-nosed litigator who let nothing stand between himself and the truth.

Criminals and CEOs alike cracked under the force of his questioning. And it was this reality that had her quietly but completely panicked.

Rafe didn't stop until he was so close she had to raise her chin to meet his gaze. As she looked up at him, Jeannie was swept away by memories of how freely they'd laughed, how fiercely they'd fought, and how fervently they'd loved.

She wanted to close the small gap between them and grab that brass ring of careless joy she had once known. She wanted to step into his arms and recapture some of those wonderful feelings she had experienced solely with him. She wanted to bury her face in the hollow of his broad shoulder and relieve herself of this heavy burden of silence she'd carried for so long.

But something perilous flickered in his eyes, as if he, too, felt the pull of the past, and it brought her to her senses.

This man, who had once held her naked under a midsummer moon and told her he loved her, had also left her without compunction and with child. Now he possessed the power to bring her world crashing down around her ears, and she would do well to watch what she said to him.

"Hello, Jeannie." His voice was deeper than she remembered, with a serrated edge of gruffness that probably served him well when examining a hostile witness.

For a split second she was tempted to turn and run for the safety of the house. She was terrified of talking to him, afraid she might inadvertently reveal something he could use against her. But telling herself that if she could just hold body and soul together for the next few minutes she'd have it made, she faced him with cool composure. "Hello, Rafe."

"It's been a while," he said.

She nodded mechanically. "It's good to see you looking so well."

"Thank you." He inclined his head at the compliment, but his mouth twisted into a mocking line that warned her he wasn't going to make this easy for her. "Or perhaps I should say, 'Thanks to you.'"

Jeannie ignored his thinly veiled gibe. In a way she'd expected it, or something like it. But she couldn't ignore the fact that Rafe was every inch the man she'd foreseen in her first and only lover.

The midnight blue of his eyes hadn't dimmed but, if anything, had become more vivid. So vivid in fact that looking into them was like receiving a jolt of electricity. Instead of serving as an insulating factor, those slashing jet brows and thick, sooty lashes intensified the force of the shock.

His features had the same bold chiseling and the same bronze coloring of her dreams, though maturity had added an emphasis on virility rather than mere handsomeness. The grooves bracketing his sensuous mouth bespoke his determination to get ahead . . . and to stay there.

The way he was dressed was a stark contrast to the past. He'd discarded the faded jeans, chambray shirts, and mud-colored boots of a college student-cum-cowhand in favor of the pinstriped suits, power ties, and polished black Cuevas of the prosperous attorney she'd always believed he would become.

It struck Jeannie as supremely ironic that, in some ways, Rafe and she had exchanged places. He'd gone on to law school and a lucrative practice, while she'd put her own college education on hold until Tony was ready to start kindergarten. And even though she had her teaching degree now, she'd really done nothing with it.

Jeannie wasn't sorry she'd made the sacrifice, however. Quite the opposite in fact. Her own mother had been ill for so many years before she died that she'd played only a shadowy role in her daughter's upbringing. So she was truly grateful for the opportunity to have given her son the time and energy that she herself had been denied.

"It was a nice turnout," Rafe said now, taking another stab at cordiality.

"Yes, it was," Jeannie agreed, thinking that

if she could just skate over the thin ice of polite conversation with him, she'd be home free.

"And a beautiful day for it too."

"Very."

A shadow fell over his angular face as he studied her. "I'd say I'm sorry—"

"But it would be a lie," she finished for him in a voice that was so soft it was barely audible.

A breeze redolent of regrets and roses swirled between them.

"How are your parents?" Though she'd never understood the reason for Maria and Antonio Martinez's middle-of-the-night departure, Jeannie had fond memories of the Circle C's former housekeeper and handyman.

"They're retired," Rafe answered tersely.

"And Olivia and Enrique?" She'd been exceptionally close to his younger sister, especially fond of his little brother, and extremely lonely after their sudden disappearance.

"Olivia is married and has two children."

"Boys or girls?" Her conscience took pains to remind her that Tony didn't even know he had cousins, much less know his cousins personally.

"One of each." He smiled like the proud uncle he was, and she thought—not for the first time, and not without a measure of sadness—what a wonderful father he would have made. "And Enrique will graduate from the university next month."

That left only Rafe, and Jeannie realized that it wouldn't do for him to know that she'd kept close tabs on him since he'd burst onto the San Antonio political scene a little over five years ago.

She read the newspapers, she watched television. She knew that he'd emerged as a strong, eloquent voice for equal justice and equal opportunity for his people. She also knew that given the hornswaggling nature of Texas politics, he would lose all credibility as a potential candidate for the state senate if it ever got out that the Hispanic hope of the nineties had fathered a child out of wedlock.

Rafe turned his gaze to Tony's receding back. "Is that your son?"

Jeannie fought to control the panic suddenly clawing at her insides. "Yes."

"Good-looking boy."

"Thank you."

He continued to monitor the trio's progress as they climbed the porch steps. "Your husband must be proud of him."

She breathed a sigh of relief when they disappeared inside the front door. "Webb isn't my husband."

"Oh?" His incisive eyes came back to her, and his black brow rose a fraction.

"But he wants to be." She knew she was treading on dangerous ground, yet she couldn't stop herself. Angry embers of his betrayal still burned in her heart, and she wanted to hurt him somehow.

Rafe flinched, confirming she'd hit her target, then recovered in the blink of an eye. "You're divorced?"

Jeannie extended her hand, hoping he'd take the hint. "Thank you for com—"

"Tell me about your husband," he encouraged, ignoring both her outstretched hand and obvious dismissal.

"My husband?" She should have remembered he was a lawyer; he picked up on other people's attempts to evade an issue.

"The man you eloped with," he reminded her silkily.

"Eloped?" She shook her head in confusion. "Who told you I eloped?"

His voice deepened to a cryptic huskiness. "I have my sources."

"Good for you," she returned in kind, fighting the urge to tell him that his "sources" were either terrible liars or totally unreliable. But if she did that, she would have to tell him the rest of the story. And she definitely didn't want to open *that* Pandora's box.

"How did you meet your husband?"

"Check with your sources."

Rafe frowned at her flippant response. "Why didn't you keep his name?"

Jeannie forced herself to smile sweetly. "Am I on trial here?"

"I'm asking the questions."

"I don't have to answer them."

His eyes narrowed with suspicion. "Did he leave you, or did—"

Her eyes smoked with anger. "That's none of your damn business!"

"You're right," he conceded reluctantly.

"I'm so glad you agree," she shot back.

"The past is dead."

But the past wasn't dead. It lived and breathed, laughed and cried, ran and jumped and rode with all the rough-and-tumble energy of a boy who would soon be ten. And the one who knew this lied through her teeth.

"Yes, the past is dead."

"As to the future—" he began.

Jeannie didn't give him a chance to finish. She spun on her heels and started to stalk away. Unfortunately she didn't get very far. Rafe came after her, grabbing her by the elbow and turning her back. She felt the sinewy pressure of his fingers through the silk of her sleeve and pulled free of his grasp. But her skin tingled with a delicious afterburn, as if it had total recall of his touch.

"Have you set a date?" he demanded.

"A date?" she echoed blankly.

The curve of his lips—she couldn't call it a real smile—caused shivers to chase along her spine. "For your wedding."

"Not yet." The instant the words were out of her mouth, she wanted to bite her tongue.

Instead she tipped her chin and, in a voice as brittle as an icicle, said, "But I'll be sure to send you an invitation."

"You do that," he countered, his voice as challenging as the gaze he fastened on her upturned face.

As an attorney Rafe had trained himself to step outside his own emotions and to think logically, to rein in his temper and let reason prevail. But logic proved a poor match for stormy gray eyes and satiny white skin. And reasoning simply failed him as he studied the full, velvety mouth that had given him so much pleasure and caused him so much pain.

Jeannie stood still for his disconcerting perusal as long as she could, then she backed up a step and said stiffly, "Well, I'd better go see to my guests."

"Take off your hat," he ordered with ominous softness.

She wasn't certain she'd heard him correctly. "I beg your pardon?"

Rafe stepped forward, forcing her to tilt her head back. Jeannie froze. His face was so close, it nearly touched hers beneath the drooping brim. The woody scent of vetiver emanated from his warm skin. Her heart—the same heart that had beat so fervently for him eleven years ago—began racing again as his blue eyes raked her over the coals of yesterday's desire.

She felt the rush of adrenaline through her

veins, heightening her senses. After all this time he still affected her—the masculine smell of him, the Dionysian force of him. She twisted her head away, then back, her lips parting with a protest that died in her throat.

"I want to see if your hair still catches sunlight." Eleven years of longing vied with eleven years of loathing in his husky voice. But it was himself he hated at that moment, not her. And what he *really* wanted tingled in the space between their lips, sending a fresh flurry of tremors down her spine.

"Some things are better left to memory," she said on a falling note.

"Not this," he drawled as his hand found the small of her back and pulled her flush against him until she felt every rigid contour of his body.

"Especially this!" she cried, determined to resist him even as the heat and the hardness of him revived passions that had too long lain dormant.

She tried to wrench free, but he held her fast. Then she wedged both of her elbows between them and bored the heels of her hands into his muscled chest, but he was not to be deflected.

Finally realizing that she was no match for his strength, she changed tactics. She looked around meaningfully, then lifted appealing eyes to his unrelenting ones. "Especially here."

"Where better?" he growled as his mouth

ground down on hers in a kiss that was as much an affirmation of life as it was an act of reclamation.

The virile length of him burned into the vulnerable softness of her as his tongue flicked persuasively over her lips, delving into the corners, tracing the tight seam she made of them, outlining their shape with silken circles until they parted on a gasp of pleasure and he finally tasted her response.

Jeannie's resistance melted into a rippling pool of pure longing as she wrapped her arms around Rafe's neck and swam toward the sleek, wet spear of his tongue. Her head tilted back sharply, her hat fell off, and her loosely pinned hair cascaded to her shoulders.

Spring sang deep inside him when he caught the fine gold strands with his free hand and felt the sun's heat captured there. Her heart tilted as she touched her tongue to his in a circling dance of rediscovery. Their bodies, having found the familiar fit of breast to chest and feminine softness to masculine hardness, swayed to a lovers' refrain from another lifetime.

"Memory didn't severe me well enough," Rafe murmured as he raised his head and tucked a stray tendril that had escaped his grasp behind her ear.

But memory served Jeannie *too* well. She had a son to protect, and Tony's interests took precedence over her own frail desires. Then there was Webb Bishop to consider. He was the last of a dying breed, a man she could rely on when the going got rough, and she knew he was waiting at home for her to say the word.

Trembling with anger at her own traitorous arousal, she slapped that stirring hand away and stepped out of those strong arms. She picked up her hat and dusted it off, then hugged it to herself. Her somber gray eyes reflected the pain of what she had to say.

"Go away, Rafe."

"We've got unfinished business, Jeannie."

"No," she denied with a vehement shake of her head. "It was finished between us eleven years ago."

"Judging by the way you kissed me back," he said softly, "we've only just begun."

"Don't confuse me with that starry-eyed girl you left behind," she warned him tightly.

His blue eyes moved up and down her slender body in a way that made her wonder if she glowed with their electric force. "You've matured into a beautiful woman."

"I've changed, all right." The excitement sputtered as she reminded herself that time heals, but scars stay. "And so have my priorities."

"Some things never change," he said, rewording her earlier argument and using it to his own advantage.

The early April breeze, heady with the scent of yellow roses and the aura of youthful passions, ruffled his sable-thick hair. Sunlight scintillated off the small silver earring that studded his left lobe. A mockingbird, perched on a nearby headstone of joined hearts, called to its mate.

"Why did you have to come back?" Jeannie could have been eighteen again, so wistfully did she ask.

"I had to see you." A muscle jumped along Rafe's clean-edged jaw. "I had to satisfy my curiosity."

"About what?"

"About the man you married."

She stiffened instinctively. "What about him?"

His lips quirked into a cynical smile. "I wanted to know what kind of man could make you forget me so easily."

"Oh . . ." She swallowed, trying to relieve the sudden dryness in her throat.

"When I first found out you'd eloped—"

"Who told you I eloped?" She reiterated the demand she'd made of him earlier.

"What difference does it make now?"

"None, I guess." Except she would have liked to know who'd spread that lie.

"Just believe me when I say I almost went out of my mind." His mouth remained in its crooked line, bitter and mocking. "Half the time I was calling myself every name in the book for not telling Big Tom to go to hell, and the other half I was congratulating myself on getting rid of the original material girl. But mostly . . ." His gaze ran over her, as if the memory were almost to painful to voice. "Mostly I was insanely jealous of the man who had you for himself."

Caught in the emotion of both the moment and his moving admission, Jeannie almost blurted out the truth. But if his expression was anything to go by, Rafe wasn't finished. And she wanted—no, she *needed*—to hear the rest of his explanation.

"I finally calmed down and decided that it was for the best." He shrugged pragmatically. "Let's face it, I wasn't exactly a hot prospect at the time—a college graduate, yes, but with no hope of ever earning enough money for law school by doing ranch work. And I realized that your new husband could probably give you more than I ever could."

Above, mare's-tail clouds pranced across a sky as bright and blue as the eyes that met and held hers. "Still, I've always wondered if he treated you as well as you deserved . . . as well as I would have."

Jeannie turned away, her silky hair swirling about her shoulders and her hands all but mangling her hat brim. She didn't want him to know how deeply affected she was by all this, didn't want him to see her face when she posed her next question. Her voice was scarcely more than a whisper as she asked, "Why did you leave me?"

Rafe didn't answer her right away—not because he didn't want to but because he didn't know where to begin. He'd come here this morning to lay the past to rest, only to find that he'd come full circle. For years he'd rued the day he'd set his sights on the girl she'd been; now he realized he wanted the woman she'd become.

But in order to have her . . .

"That's a long story," he said at last. "And this is neither the time nor the place to tell it."

Her pulse fluttered when she felt his fingers close in on her elbow and assert a guiding pressure toward the wrought-iron gate. "What are you doing?"

"I'm walking you back to the house."

"But . . ." Stunned by his declaration, Jeannie faltered slightly, breaking the purposeful rhythm of their steps and throwing Rafe offstride as well.

His grip tightened in support. "We need to talk."

"I really don't have time today." She shook her head, partly in feeble protest to his suggestion and partly in sheer amazement at the speed with which things were moving.

"Give me ten minutes," Rafe bargained, in the firm baritone that had swayed its fair share of juries.

Ten minutes? Jeannie's heart threatened to beat its way out of her chest as their steps crunched along the gravel drive that led to the house. Ten minutes could destroy her!

Three

"Where's Tony?" Jeannie demanded of Webb the instant they entered the house.

Rafe heard the anxious note in her voice and chalked it up to maternal concern. Personally he'd always been of the opinion that Big Tom would have to hire someone to cry at his funeral. But the tears that had streamed down the boy's cheeks had been the product of genuine grief. And though he couldn't imagine it, he had to wonder if the Archie Bunker of Bolero had actually mellowed in his old age.

"Tony's in the kitchen." Webb had obviously been haunting the entry hall, waiting for her. Now his brown eyes seemed unusually bright as they skimmed from her bare head and unbound hair to her flushed face. "Rusty promised to take him riding as soon as he's finished eating."

Jeannie fingered the brim of the hat she still held and self-consciously wet her lips. She tasted Rafe's kiss on them and experienced the ridiculous but not unfounded fear that it might be visible. Belatedly remembering her manners, she introduced the men who stood on either side of her.

"Dr. Webb Bishop," she said briskly, "I'd like you to meet Rafe Martinez."

Rafe extended his hand. "Dr. Bishop."

"Mr. Martinez." Webb sounded as if the words had been forced from his throat.

The two men shook hands, sizing each other up as potential rivals for Jeannie's affection. Rafe was taller and darker than Webb, but they were both professionals, both successful in their chosen fields of endeavor. The tension built and the low buzz of background conversations seemed as loud as the roar of a blue norther while they quietly assessed each other's chances.

Standing between them, seeing the tanned hand that had once known her intimately clasping the fairer one that knew her in only the most superficial manner, she suddenly felt like the rope in a tug-of-war.

"If you'll excuse me," she said, removing herself from the highly charged situation as gracefully as she could, "I'm going to check on

Tony and freshen up before I see to my guests."

Rafe and Webb dropped their hands and all pretense of propriety, turning of one accord to study her ashen face.

"I'll catch up with you later," Rafe said, the rumbling tautness in his voice making it sound like a threat.

"Fine," she agreed, unable to bring herself to meet Webb's silently appealing expression. Taking the coward's way out, she headed for the safety of the kitchen and the reassuring sight of her son . . . of Rafe's son.

The country kitchen, spanning the rear of the house, was papered in a small floral of blues and greens and creams. Six-inch pine flooring shone spotlessly. A trestle table surrounded by comfortable arrowback chairs invited people to sit and share a meal. Tea tins lining the soffits over the oak cupboards lent charm, and a bread-making board under one of the windows meant business.

Tony had already changed out of his dark suit and good shoes into play clothes, boots, and the neon-blue baseball cap he would have worn around the clock if Jeannie would have let him. He was happily ensconced at the head of the table, a plate with a half-eaten taco and a glass of milk sitting before him.

"Hi, Mom," he said around a mouthful of taco.

"Hi, honey." She put her arm around his shoulder and planted a kiss on his freshly scrubbed cheek, relishing the spring of his flesh and the familiar bump and blade of bone.

By nature Big Tom had been all rough edges and emotional reserve. In contrast Laurrinda had been all parties and perfume and pitiable need. The social butterfly whose wings had been clipped by cancer. And by the time Jeannie was born, it had essentially been over between them.

To this day she didn't really understand what had drawn her parents together in the first place. If she'd had to guess, she would have said it was a classic case of opposites attracting. But somewhere along the line the magnetism, not to mention the marriage, had lost its pull.

It was their remoteness, though, that was responsible for Jeannie having made a daily habit of hugging her son and saying to him the words she'd seldom heard when she was growing up . . . the words she whispered now into his clean-smelling hair. "I love you."

Tony swallowed and said, "I love you too."

Knowing he wouldn't sit still for much more of this "mush"—his word, not hers—she let him go and turned to look at the woman who'd taken Maria Martinez's place as cook and housekeeper. "How's it going, Martha?"

A gaunt, gray-haired woman who'd never married and who had no children of her own, Martha Spencer ruled her culinary realm with a spatula, an iron skillet, and the firm belief that food was the panacea for all the problems in this world. Toward that end she'd been cooking for three days straight, preparing a proper send-off for Big Tom.

Martha had never met Rafe, of course, but Rusty had obviously filled her in. Her hazel eyes telegraphed a visual missive that she was doing her part to protect Tony even as she added her vocal assurance. "So far, so good."

"I'm going to write down the calf count for Rusty," Tony said excitedly. Like the majority of the children who grew up on a ranch, he equated chores and the care of the animals with fun. "That way we'll know what we're going to need in the way of supplies when branding starts next week."

"Great." Jeannie smiled at his enthusiasm. Big Tom had started early with his grandson, training him to take over the Circle C someday, teaching him the importance of each and every job, instilling a love of the land in his heart and soul. That Tony was so ready and willing to work on the day of his funeral was perhaps the rancher's greatest legacy.

"You're not going anywhere until you finish your lunch, young man," Martha interjected in an imperious but loving tone.

Tony wolfed down the rest of his taco and reached for his glass of milk. He drained it in one long swallow, then took an ineffectual swipe at the white mustache it left on his upper lip with the back of his hand. That done, he got up from the table and dashed for the back door and the most direct route to the barn.

"See ya later, Mom," he called over his shoulder.

Before Jeannie could even open her mouth to say good-bye, he'd closed the door behind him. Tony seemed to be going through a phase where he had to race at everything. Sometimes, especially toward the end of a long day, she felt like the tortoise trying to keep up with the hare.

Shaking her head in silent amusement, she asked Martha, "Is there anything you need me to take to the dining room?"

The older woman shook her head and began clearing the kitchen table. "Rusty carried the last of it out while I was making Tony's taco."

"If you need any help, call me," Jeannie offered before pushing through the swinging doors that led to the dining room.

The table had been extended to its full length and set with duplicate lines of serving dishes for smooth traffic flow. A portable bar stood in one corner, and the French doors leading to the patio had been thrown open so that the guests could eat in umbrella-shaded comfort by the swimming pool.

Martha had done herself proud in the food department, combining the finest Southwest specialties with the best of Hill Country cooking.

The mirror over the sideboard reflected silver ramekins of heuvos rancheros rubbing elbows with chafing dishes full of their fluffy scrambled counterpart. Bite-sized pieces of chorizo shared platter space with crispy cuts of country ham. Clay steamers kept stacks of tortillas warm alongside baskets of beaten biscuits. Bowls of spicy gaucamole backed up to boats of cream gravy. Dessert plates mounded with honey-laced sopaipillas and butter-rich sugar cookies brought up the rear.

But food was the last thing on Jeannie's mind. Rafe's surprise appearance at the funeral, his kiss and her response to it, the terrible threat he posed where Tony was concerned . . . Everything had happened so fast, she needed some time alone to think. So after weathering a few more well-meant condolences and encouraging people to eat heartily, she slipped upstairs to her bedroom.

She closed the door, shutting out the hum of conversation downstairs. Then she closed her eyes, and for a moment she was eighteen again, lying in her canopy bed on a hot July night, tingling with anticipation as she waited for the *thunk* of a rock against the window screen, feeling herself cross the invisible line from girl to woman when the signal came and she snuck down the stairs, out the front door, and into Rafe's loving arms.

The room had been redecorated since then, the teenager's clutter having given way to artfully arranged family treasures, and the canopy bed having been replaced by an antique cherry four-poster. But those memories and others swirled around her now, dancing like dust motes in the shafts of sunshine streaming through the lace-clad windows.

As she put her hat back in its flowered box on the closet shelf, Jeannie couldn't help but recall how carefully she'd chosen the white sundress she'd worn for their first night together, how nervously she'd done up the dainty buttons that covered her breasts and how deftly Rafe had undone them, how tenderly he'd lowered her to the moonlit grass and made her his.

Determined not to dwell on the past, Jeannie stepped to her dresser and repinned her hair before wandering restlessly to the window that overlooked the ranch yard and parting the curtains. But as the breeze picked up and she watched the dust rise off the gravel drive, the past came back to her in a rush of images. . . .

She could see Rafe behind the wheel of the Studebaker he'd repainted a dark blue and commuted to and from college in. She could hear him gunning the motor once—his secret "I'm home" to her—before he killed it. She could smell his powerful masculine scent and feel his strong arms holding her as they'd lain in the backseat, planning for that distant day when they could bring their love out in the open and face the world as one.

His sexuality—sharp as musk—had filled her senses, blinding her to their different cultural backgrounds and religious beliefs, deafening her to Big Tom's warnings to steer clear of "that damn greaser" and his dire threats of what would happen if she didn't. She'd muted her own desire to shout back "I love him!" and had worried constantly that she would be caught sneaking out to keep their secret assignations. She would have risked anything, even her father's wrath, to be with Rafe.

But one night she had waited for his signal in vain. The luminous hands on her bedside clock had crawled toward dawn as she'd kept her lonely vigil. Eventually she'd given up on seeing him and cried herself to sleep.

The next morning, when she awoke to find him gone, something inside her had died. And something else had lived.

"Jeannie?"

At the sound of Webb's muted voice and sharp knock she snapped back to the present, surprised to find that only minutes had passed instead of years. She spun away from the window just as he opened the door.

In the few seconds it took to reorient herself, Webb's eyes circled the room that he, like Rafe, had never set foot in. He took in everything, from the fringed Turkish carpet that covered the parquet floor, to the Victorian dollhouse she'd found in the attic and refurbished, to the Bakelite accessories that served as her vanity set. For some reason it rankled to think he should be the first to see the heirlooms she held so dear.

Nodding as if to say he approved of her eclectic taste, his gaze moved back to her, standing beside the window. "I've been looking everywhere for you."

"I'm sorry." A guilty flush crept up her face, as if she'd been caught doing something indecent. "I just needed to get away from the noise and the crowd."

"I understand," he said soothingly.

"Is something wrong?" she asked, thinking of Tony now.

"No." He smiled his steady smile, putting her fears on that front to rest. "I just wanted to say good-bye."

"Good-bye?" She looked at him with a blank expression.

Webb patted the beeper that he wore on his belt and that connected him to the hospital. "Duty pages."

Jeannie dared not think how relieved she was that she wouldn't be torn between him and Rafe the rest of the day. Her nerves were already stretched as taut as the exercise trampoline that sat in the corner. Any more stress and they'd snap.

"Come on." Fixing a smile on her face, she crossed the room and took his arm. "I'll walk you downstairs."

At the front door he captured her hands in his warm, somewhat damp ones and gazed down at her with a slightly desperate expression. "It didn't seem right to say this when Big Tom was so ill, but now . . . I'm falling in love with you, Jeannie."

"Oh, Webb . . ." she said softly, moved in spite of herself by the knowledge that she could so easily break his heart.

He released her hands and took hold of her shoulders. "I'd be good to you. And I'd treat Tony like my own son. You have my word on that."

She realized then that he was drowning in false hopes as she was drowning in fear of exposure, and she didn't know how to save either one of them.

A muscle twitched below his eye as his mouth came down on hers, and he kissed her with a passion she sorely wished she could match. The problem was—

"I'll call you later," he promised, his breath coming hard when the kiss ended.

"Do that," she agreed, her breathing as calm as if she'd just awakened from a good night's sleep.

No sooner had she closed the front door than Rusty came up behind her. His face wore a terribly worried expression and his tone crackled with urgency as he asked the question Jeannie had asked Webb earlier. "Where's Tony?"

In addition to the outside entrance from the porch, Big Tom's office was accessible by a set of pocket doors that opened off the dining room.

Having made all the small talk he could stand, and holding a Bloody Maria that he'd barely tasted, Rafe wandered into the walnut-paneled office.

A massive century-old desk, its burled wood accented with heavy brass trappings, dominated the room. A gun cabinet stood against the far wall, gleaming rifle barrels showing through its locked glass door. And the memory of his fateful meeting with Big Tom seemed to echo off the walls. . . .

"Sit down, son." The rancher had looked up from the ledger book on his desk with an expression that was anything but inviting. He indicated with a brusque nod of his head one of the leather armchairs normally reserved for his cronies.

Rafe's instincts, already on red alert, had screamed a warning when he'd heard the word *son*. It was odd enough that he'd been summoned to the rancher's inner sanctum. But not once in the six years he'd been living and working on the ranch had Big Tom ever called him—to his face anyway—anything but "boy."

"I'll stand," he'd said politely, preferring to face calamity on his feet.

Big Tom had shrugged, as if to say, "Suit yourself." Then he'd closed the ledger book and cut straight to the chase. "There's two things you don't mess with, boy." He'd also reverted to type. "One is a man's mind, and the other is his daughter."

Rafe had known then that Jeannie's father had found them out. He'd known, too, that the wealthy rancher would spend every dime at his disposal, call in every favor at his command, pull every string at his fingertips, in order to keep his daughter from marrying a migrant worker's son.

"I love her," he'd declared, his muscles coiling for action and the blood singing in his veins as he'd geared up for the showdown.

"Love—the great equalizer," Big Tom had scoffed before reaching for one of the specially blended cigars that he'd kept in the silver humidor that sat at his elbow.

Rafe had been vaguely startled to realize that this wasn't just about Jeannie. He loved her with all his heart, and he'd always hated the sneaking around because he felt it cheapened their relationship, making it something to be ashamed of rather than something to be celebrated.

But he'd also had a bellyful of backing away, of being treated as less than human because he was Hispanic, of watching his parents bow and scrape to the Anglos in general and to this Anglo in particular.

The air in the office had been as sulfurous as the match that lit the cigar, as electric as the atmosphere before a tornado, as tense as a standoff.

Without breaking eye contact, Big Tom had lazed back in the desk's companion swivel chair and clamped the cigar butt between his teeth. And then, with the richly fragrant tobacco smoke rising above his head like a cloud and a knife edge of hardness underlying his smooth voice, he'd proceeded to make Rafe an offer he couldn't possibly refuse.

"'Scuse me."

The polite young voice jerked Rafe back to the present. He shook off the galling reverie and turned to see Jeannie's son fidgeting in the doorway. But as he searched the juvenile face, he couldn't shake the feeling that he'd seen it before today.

"What's wrong?" he asked.

The boy grinned sheepishly. "I forgot something."

"Where is it?"

"In the desk." The boy took off his hat, sprouting a cowlick. "But if you're busy or something, I can come back for it later."

Rafe smiled at his obvious reluctance to leave empty-handed. "Come and get it."

"Gee, thanks."

Except for that fleeting sense of recognition at the gravesite, Rafe hadn't really given Jeannie's son much thought. And even though he'd heard his name a couple of times, he was ashamed to admit he couldn't remember it.

Now he turned his full attention to the boy, his eyes skimming the rebellious mop of dark hair and the youth-softened yet strongly chiseled lines of his profile as he stepped to the desk, opened the lap drawer, and began rifling through it.

"What did you forget?" Rafe swirled the contents of his glass, then drained it in one long swallow. The combination of vodka and jalapeño-flavored tomato juice burned away the bad taste that Big Tom's memory had left in his mouth.

"This." Jeannie's son smiled and held up an ivory-handled pocketknife, its blade safely closed. A gangly mixture of arms and legs, his serious blue eyes struck a kindred chord in the man observing his actions. "Grandpa said I could have it if anything happened to him."

Bothered by something he couldn't identify to save his soul, Rafe narrowed his study of the boy. "What's your name?"

"Tony Crane," he said as he shut the drawer.

Crane.

Some cold premonition clenched at Rafe's guts as he remembered Jeannie's evasive response when he'd asked her why she hadn't kept her husband's name. It couldn't be, and yet . . .

"How old are you?" he demanded now.

"Ten." And then the boy qualified his answer with, "Well, I'm almost ten."

"When's your birthday?"

"April twenty-fifth."

Time stopped moving forward for Rafe as he recalled those long-ago midsummer nights. He recalled, too, that Jeannie had seemed more disconcerted than defensive when he'd mentioned her elopement.

Something in his intense expression must have spooked Tony because he began slowly backing toward the door. "Well, I've gotta go now."

Rafe nodded, his eyes never leaving that more-familiar-by-the-minute face.

Tony wasn't so nervous, though, that he forgot the manners his mother had drilled into him. At the door he paused and said, "Nice to meet you, Mr. . . . ?"

"Martinez."

"Martinez," Tony repeated before he took off.

Damning Jeannie and the SOB who'd fathered her in the same sizzling breath, Rafe followed the boy into the dining room.

His footsteps slowed as he watched Tony stop and take a sugar cookie off one of the plates on the table. His eyes hardened to ice when he caught a glimpse of two faces, one a clone of his own, in the mirror above the sideboard. His ears roared as the truth hit him with the power of a freight train.

Fear drove a stake through Jeannie's heart as she stood in the entry hall, gripping the brass door handle and staring apprehensively at Rusty. "I thought Tony was with you!"

"He was."

"What happened?"

"My horse came up with a limp, so I had to saddle another one." Rusty's battered straw Stetson shaded his sun-leathered face, and a tin of snuff shone through the pocket of the shirt he'd changed into after the funeral. "Tony was looking for a piece of wood to whittle while he waited—"

Jeannie snapped her fingers. "Big Tom's pocketknife."

Rusty shook his head in self-disgust. "I should've known."

"You see if he's gone back out to the barn," she ordered as she turned on her heel. "I'll check in the office."

Her search ended when she entered the dining room. Her eyes went dark with despair when she saw Rafe standing behind Tony at the table. Her heart hit rock bottom when she looked into the mirror over the sideboard to find two faces, one a perfect miniature of the other, reflected in its silvery surface.

Four

My son, Rafe thought, his swelling pride undercut by the painful realization that he'd been played for a fool. Tony is my son, and she never told me . . . never intended to tell me.

In suspense, Jeannie watched his face. At first she read incredulity, then enlightenment, then finally an intense rage. While she deeply regretted that he'd had to find out like this, she also felt relieved that the truth was out at long last.

Their eyes, his burning with an arctic brilliance and hers misting with hot tears, met in the mirror for an ephemeral moment. Once, a passing glance was enough to set her soul afire and her body aflame. Now she shook under the piercing accusation reflected there.

Jeannie was the first to look away, her gaze

veering to Tony, then back to Rafe. Her be-
seeching expression asked him not to create a
scene in front of their son; his barely percep-
tible nod assured her that he would keep this
between the two of them for the time being.

She took him at his silent word, stepping
up to the table to put a possessive hand on
Tony's shoulder and saying lightly, "There you
are."

He turned, the pocketknife and his cap in
one hand and a half-eaten cookie in the other.
"Oh, hi, Mom."

"Rusty's been looking everywhere for you,"
she chided him in a mild tone.

"Gosh, I hope he wasn't worried about me."
Tony frowned in sincere contrition. "I just
came back to get Grandpa's pocketknife."

"And a cookie." Her voice held no rebuke as
she smiled down at the sugary treat.

He grinned, obviously relieved to hear that
he wasn't in serious trouble, and put his hat
back on. "I'd better go catch up with Rusty,
huh?"

She nodded. "He's waiting for you in the
barn."

Rafe had remained stationary to this point.
Now he set his empty glass on the sideboard
and grabbed hold of her wrist, his fingers
clamping around it like a manacle.

Jeannie stiffened but she didn't pull away.
She understood the silent message conveyed
by his detaining hand. Tony could leave, but

she was to stay. She felt hot and cold all at the same time, dreading the conversation that was to come yet hoping to finally set the record straight.

"Why don't you take some of those cookies with you?" Rafe's calm tone belied the angry vibrations emanating from him like a force field, charging the air around him.

"Take some for Rusty too," Jeannie encouraged, fighting to keep her voice on an even keel.

Tony seemed oblivious to the brittle tension between the two adults, but he knew a good idea when he heard one. He stuck the knife in his jeans pocket, stuffed another cookie in his mouth, then grabbed as many more as he could carry in one trip.

"Rusty went out the front door," Jeannie told him as he started for the kitchen.

He braked on a dime and changed direction.

Rafe tightened his hold on Jeannie's wrist and dragged her along behind him. She stumbled in her high heels and gasped his name, but it did her no good. He neither slowed down nor relieved the painful pressure of his fingers until they reached the kitchen. And then he let up only slightly.

Martha was loading the dishwasher when they barged in on her. She looked from Rafe's formidable expression to Jeannie's fatalistic one and closed the machine.

"I'll go gather up the rest of the dirty dishes." She took a tray to carry them on, then stopped at the door and looked back at Jeannie. "But I'll just be in shouting distance if you need me for anything.

As the door swung closed behind her, Rafe spun on Jeannie and jerked her toward him, facing her furiously.

He towered above her, his expression as hard and vengeful as a bandido's and his eyes as hot and blue as a flame. There was an aura of coiled violence about him, a savage quality in the ruthlessly molded line of his jaw and mouth that was totally at odds with his otherwise civilized appearance.

Jeannie quailed beneath his fierce stare but kept her own expression defiant. She'd had too many years of practice in holding up her head, of leading with her chin in the face of censure. And she didn't have to cower before any man, even if he was Tony's father.

"He's my son, isn't he?" he accused.

"He's *my* son!" she said adamantly.

"You know damned good and well what I mean," he retorted with deadly calm. "I'm his father."

"You're nothing to him," she returned cruelly. "You're just some stranger who showed up for his grandfather's funeral."

His reaction made her die a little inside. His head snapped back, as if she'd slapped his face. His nostrils flared on a stunned breath.

His eyes darkened momentarily as something like pain clouded their depths.

Jeannie longed to reach out and caress that rigid jaw, to take away the hurt. She wished she could snatch back the hateful words she'd so callously thrown at him. She wondered what had happened to the love they had known, the promises they had made, the life they had planned.

"Rafe—" she began, but it was too late.

"Husband be damned," he snarled harshly. "You've probably never even been married."

"I never said I was," she cried in self-defense. "You just assumed—"

"But you sure as hell let me believe it, didn't you?" He flung her wrist away then, as if he couldn't bear to touch her.

"Yes," she admitted without apology.

"Why?" he demanded through clenched teeth.

"I was afraid."

"Afraid of what?"

She rubbed the slender wrist he'd just released, more as a stalling ploy than in accusation. He saw the bruises that were already beginning to form on her soft white skin—bruises that his own steely brown fingers had caused—and a surge of male protectiveness swept over him, leaving him shaken and disgusted with himself.

"Did I hurt you?" he demanded tersely.

She dropped her arm. "No."

"You're lying."

"What difference does it make?"

"What do you mean by that?"

She tilted her head at its haughtiest angle. "It's what you wanted to hear."

His eyes hardened to cold blue marble. "I guess it was, at that."

For a long moment they simply stared at each other.

Behind them lay a passion that, for better or worse, had never cooled. Between them stood a child conceived of their love. Ahead of them loomed a potential custody battle that could prove bitter, brutal.

"How could you do this to me?" he suddenly roared.

"Shout it to the world, why don't you?" she yelled back.

"Answer me, damn you." He lowered his voice to a sinister whisper. "How could you do this to me?"

"You're a fine one to talk!"

"Don't give me that garbage."

"Who left who?"

The silence that followed Jeannie's heated demand was filled with pain. It glittered in gray eyes and blue. And it was physically etched on both her face and his. But when he spoke again, Rafe's words reflected neither the grief nor the regret that each of them felt.

"My name's been in the newspaper at least once a week for the last five years."

"Congratulations."

He ignored her snide compliment and went

on coldly. "I've spoken at dozens of large rallies. Hundreds of small—"

"So?" She nearly choked on her challenge.

"So you've known where I was all this time." His hands worked in vivid concert with his voice, cutting to the heart of the matter. "So you could've called me and told me I'd fathered a child."

Jeannie sidestepped that for the moment. "I tried to find you right after you left."

"I'll just bet," Rafe scoffed.

"I called everyone I could think of—your relatives, your friends. I even went into the barrio, thinking you'd gone back there. And then . . ." She swallowed hard, the memory of those dreadful days coming back to her with sickening clarity. "Then the nausea hit me, and I had to tell Big Tom."

His jaw bunched with a fury too long contained. "Did he tell you in return that he'd offered to pay off my college loans and pick up the tab for my law school tuition if I promised to leave the ranch and never contact you again?"

She recoiled in shock and anger. "I don't believe you!"

Unperturbed, he went on. "And did he tell you that when I refused his offer, he threatened to report my family to the immigration authorities if we didn't pack up and clear out?"

"But you were born in San Antonio." She

knew that that automatically made him an American citizen.

"Olivia and Enrique and I were, yes."

She was almost afraid to ask. "And your parents . . . ?"

He confirmed her worst fears. "Mexican nationals who'd illegally crossed the border looking for work and then stayed to raise a family."

Jeannie shook her head in frantic denial, as if doing so would negate everything he'd just said.

Rafe took a step closer, his eyes narrowing to menacing slits. "Last but not least, did he tell you that when I called the ranch a month after we left, he dropped the bombshell that you'd eloped?"

"No," she said softly, still shaking her head.

He nodded his. "Yes."

"But . . ." Struggling against this new betrayal, she tried one last time to clear Big Tom's name. "He said he'd help me look for you. He even said he'd call the sheriff and have him try to track you down."

He laughed mirthlessly. "With all his money and all his connections, don't you think he could have found me if he'd really wanted to?"

She had no answer for him, and in the ensuing silence even the clock on the wall seemed to mock her naïveté.

Tick . . . How could she have been so blind as to overlook a lifetime of prejudice on Big Tom's part? *Tock* . . . How could she have been so stupid as to believe he would really pull out the stops to help her locate Rafe? *Tick* . . .

Oh, if only she could turn back time!

"Five years!" Rafe finally addressed the issue she had managed to avoid earlier. "You could have told me five years ago that I'd fathered a son, and you didn't!"

Near panic, Jeannie raised her palms in a conciliatory gesture. "If you would just listen to me—"

"So you can tell me some more of your lies?"

"I've never lied to you!"

"Except by omission."

She lowered her hands and glanced down at the floor, knowing her actions were as good as admissions of guilt. But she refused to damn herself further by offering lame explanations.

He captured her chin between his thumb and forefinger, forcing her head up so that he could see her face. The blue of his eyes burned into hers before blazing a fiery trail down her cheeks to her lips, moist and trembling.

A dizzying sense of déjà vu enveloped them, and she half-expected his mouth to smother hers in another kiss.

Her mind rebelled against the idea, given the animosity between them, but her body had a memory of its own. It recalled instead the gentle caress of his hands upon her breasts and their aching crests, the spreading warmth of his palms sliding down her belly to the juncture of her thighs, the ball of his thumb bringing her to the brink of oblivion, the muscular length of him weighing her down and driving her over the edge.

Even now, with both of them up in arms over their son, desire for him flickered deep inside her.

He doused the flames with his icy demand. "Why didn't you come to me? Write to me? Call me?"

Irritated with herself, she wrenched her chin from his fingers. "A million reasons."

"Name one."

"I wasn't sure you'd believe me," she confessed around a deep breath.

"All I'd have had to do was look at him to know you were telling the truth."

Her eyes appealed to him for understanding. "I couldn't take that chance."

He regarded her dispassionately. "Name another."

"I was afraid you'd try to get back at me through Tony."

"How?"

"By taking out your anger toward me on him."

"Hurting him, you mean."

Jeannie nodded miserably. "Yes."

Rafe exploded with rage. "For five years you deliberately hid my son's existence from me, then you have the unmitigated gall to stand there and tell me you did it because you thought I'd hurt him—my own flesh and blood!"

"I wasn't sure how you'd react when you found out," she snapped. While his outrage now made her fears seem foolish in retrospect, they'd haunted her all this time.

He took a deep breath, controlling his temper by an act of will. "And how else did you justify keeping me in the dark for all these years?"

"Your political career."

That made him pause. Running for the state senate was something he'd been preparing for since he'd gotten out of law school. Toward that end, he'd built a potent political base within the barrio, winning local battles over housing and better drainage on the low-lying West Side.

Now he wanted to cross the fault line from Mesoamerican presence to mainstream politician. He wanted to tackle the statewide issues, such as public education and health care, that affected Anglo and Hispanic alike. And even though the primary was still a year away, he'd already hired someone to raise the money and generate the name-recognition he needed to run his campaign.

This wasn't exactly the kind of publicity he'd had in mind, however. And just thinking about the newspaper headlines alone—thinking aloud, really—was enough to make him groan. "The media would have me for breakfast, lunch, and dinner if this story got out."

"It wouldn't be any picnic for Tony either," she said pointedly.

Rafe nodded in agitated agreement, then nailed her in place with a hard stare. "This could have been cleared up quietly if you'd only gotten in touch with me when you found out where I was."

Sick to her bones of all the deceptions, Jeannie told it like it was. "By then it was too late, and I was too bitter."

"I had a right to know."

"You had no rights as far as I was concerned."

His hand slammed down on the tabletop, making her jump. "Who the hell appointed you judge, jury, and executioner?"

The door swung open at the loud crash, and Martha looked in from the dining room. Jeannie warded her off with a shake of her head, and the door swung closed.

Rafe paced the kitchen floor like a caged panther, cursing her father under his breath, mourning the years he'd lost with his son, trying to think how to handle this so that no one else would be hurt. His hair gleamed blue-black in the sunlight shafting through the sparkling windows, and his shoulders threw broad shadows across the shining wood floor.

Jeannie followed closely on his heels, wanting to reach out and cradle his head to her breast to ease his torment. She wished with every fiber of her being that they could go back to the beginning and make a fresh start, and wondered how she could undo the damage that Big Tom had done.

When he stopped abruptly, she collided with him from behind. And when he whirled on her, she fell back a step, feeling powerless to cope with the raw pain she saw in his eyes.

"You're as manipulative as your old man." His accusation pierced her like a well-aimed arrow.

She stiffened in shock and affront at the vicious comparison. She certainly didn't blame him for feeling that way—his scorn was well founded in fact—but it still hurt her to the core that he thought she was capable of such machinations.

"That's neither true nor fair," she declared fiercely.

"He couldn't have a son of his own, so he took mine."

"He loved Tony."

"You thought you could just kiss me off—"

"You kissed me!"

"Consider us even, then." He closed the gap between them, and she could feel both the heat of his anger and the fabric of his trousers through her silk skirt. "You used me and I used you."

Her gray eyes widened in dismay. Her throat went itchy and tight with emotion. Her heart ached at the way he'd just ground the kiss they'd shared at the gravesite under the heel of retaliation.

Rafe gripped her shoulders and shook her, hard. "When are you going to tell Tony about me?"

Jeannie twisted, but couldn't escape his digging fingers. "When I feel he can handle it."

"If you think I'm going to let another day go by without claiming my son, *Señorita* Crane," he stressed with a mocking accent, "you've got another think coming."

She felt a cold chill at the realization that he could take legal action regarding Tony. "But you can't just pop into his life after ten years and expect to take charge."

"I'm his father!" He released her suddenly, and she stumbled backward. "I have rights!"

She caught her balance against the back of a chair and drew herself up rigidly. "You have no rights—not like this!"

His blue eyes bored through her like a diamond-point drill. "Don't bet the ranch on it."

Maternal instinct transformed Jeannie into a tigress, turning her into as dangerous an adversary as he. "I'll see you in hell before I let you turn Tony's world upside down."

"Fine." Rafe spun on his heel and strode across the room. At the door he pivoted and fired his parting shot. "I'll see you in court."

Five

The special-delivery letter came three days later.

No sooner had Jeannie returned from taking Tony to school and sat down at the desk in the office—her office now—to write the last of the thank-you notes and to pay the vet and hay bills than she heard the mail truck pull into the ranch yard.

Her fine brows drew into a frown as she got to her feet and went to the window. The Circle C was on a rural route, which meant the mail was usually deposited in the box at the end of the drive. She picked it up when she brought Tony home from school. She really couldn't think of a reason for the sudden change in routine . . . unless . . .

With a sense of foreboding so powerful it

squeezed the breath from her lungs, she went out the door and down the porch steps to sign for the letter.

Jeannie stared at the creamy vellum envelope with the return address embossed in the upper left-hand corner for a long time before she tore it open. Her heart sank to new depths of despair as she read Rafe's demand for parental visitation rights. This was just the beginning, she realized. Next he very well might try to take Tony away from her.

"Bad news?" Rusty had gotten a late start on riding herd that morning, claiming "Old Art," as he referred to his chronic arthritis, had kept him up half the night. His spurs, which bore his initials in silver, jingled as he led his bay across the ranch yard on legs that had grown a little stiffer and a little less agile with every passing year.

"See for yourself." Jeannie handed him the letter, then pressed her fingertips to her temples, attempting to ease a sledgehammer of a headache that gave new meaning to the word *pain*. She hadn't been sleeping well, either, but not because of a physical problem. Every time she climbed into bed and closed her eyes, the emotions that Rafe's kiss and subsequent statement had aroused in her came back to haunt her.

Obviously they had a sexual chemistry that wouldn't quit. He had only to touch her and she caught fire; he had only to tell her how he felt and she practically melted into a puddle at his feet. But she had to ask herself how much of their desire was rooted in nostalgia. She also had to wonder whether the question was moot now that he'd found out about Tony.

Jeannie realized that Rafe probably hated the Cranes with a passion. And with good reason, she had to admit. One had run him off the ranch, and one had robbed him of precious years of his son's life. Now he was going to extract his revenge, and unless she wanted a messy court battle with Tony in the middle, she was going to have to pay.

Rusty's bay snorted restlessly in the silence, eager to get moving. Dust clouded the horizon as cowhands herded prime beef toward the holding pens. A pregnant mare, her abdomen swollen to twice its normal size, munched tender sprigs of green grass in the pasture.

Nature quickened in spring, as did the ranchwork—sorting cattle, branding calves, and catching foals. Add to that the task of keeping up with Tony and the business of settling Big Tom's estate, and Jeannie hadn't had time to discuss what she had learned the day of the funeral with Rusty.

"You knew all along that Big Tom had sent Rafe away, didn't you?" she whispered when he finished the letter and handed it back to her.

There was a short pause before he answered. "He didn't come right out and tell me what he'd done, but it didn't take long for me to figure it out."

"Why, Rusty?" She choked on a sob, as always demanding from him the answers she couldn't find elsewhere. "Why did he do it?"

As spare with words as he was in appearance, the old cowboy said succinctly, "He was trying to protect you."

"In the long run he punished me—and Tony too."

"He thought the sun rose and set in that boy."

She hid her bitterness behind a sardonic smile. "He was so desperate for a male heir, he was even willing to overlook the fact that Tony's father was Hispanic."

Rusty seemed disinclined to speak ill of the dead. "Aren't you judging him a little harshly?"

"Harshly?" Jeannie was in neither an understanding nor a forgiving mood. "By rights I ought to hate him."

"There's no hate in you—only grief." He dropped the reins and gently gathered her into his arms, their embrace speaking volumes about the strong bond between them.

Big Tom had given Jeannie her first horse, but it was the red-headed Rusty who'd taught her to ride, then wiped her tears and told her to get right back up in the saddle when she was thrown. And it was Rusty, grinning as proudly as any father there, who'd taken her to those barrel-racing contests she'd competed in as a child and cheered her on to victory.

Her mother had thought the world of him too. Laurrinda Crane might have been Big

Tom's beautiful blond wife, but within months of his hiring on as ranch manager of the Circle C, Rusty Pride would have walked barefoot over barbed wire for the former debutante from San Antonio.

There had hardly been a day that Laurrinda hadn't called on the cowboy to run some errand that her husband was too busy or too dadblamed impatient to do. Once, years ago, when Big Tom had gone to a cattle auction, she had even asked Rusty to help her host an old-fashioned barbecue for the planning committee for the Bluebonnet Ball, one of the most prestigious social events of the season. Big Tom had gotten back in time to escort his wife to the ball, of course, but Jeannie would never forget how eagerly Rusty had danced attention on her mother the night of the cookout.

Laurrinda had counted on him more than ever toward the end. When the lump in her breast was pronounced both malignant and metastatic, it was Rusty—not Big Tom—who'd sat on the porch with her on a summer evening while she voiced her fear of dying. When the radiation treatments robbed her of her luxuriant hair, it was Rusty—not Big Tom—who'd told her that what was on a woman's mind was more important than what was on her head. And when the breath left her body and they laid her in her grave, it was Rusty—not Big Tom—who'd taken her sobbing daughter into his arms and held her, much as he held her now.

Jeannie buried her face in his shirtfront and wept for the first time since the funeral— for the loving father she wished she'd had and for the lanky foreman who'd done such a commendable job of filling his shoes. She cried for hopes dashed and dreams shattered. And finally, because she was so confused and hurt and tired, she cried for herself.

"Feel better?" Rusty asked when the storm subsided.

"Yes." Surprisingly enough, she did.

He released her and picked up the reins. "What now?"

"I don't know." She put the letter back in the envelope, then lifted her chin at a defiant angle. "But if Rafe thinks he can take Tony away from me, he's wrong. If he tries, I'll hire the best lawyers money can buy and go after him tooth and nail."

"Spoken like a true Crane."

Rusty was right of course. She sounded just like Big Tom at his worst. What she couldn't control, she wanted to crush. But what was she supposed to do—lie down and let Rafe steamroll her in a court of law?

"All I want to do is keep my son," she retorted in her own defense.

"Your son *and* Rafe's son."

Guiltily she glanced away.

"How did you feel," he pressed, "to find someone you loved had hidden something so important from you?"

Betrayed was too pale a word for how she felt about Big Tom's treachery. She longed to scream and release her pain, but what would that change? Nothing—nothing at all.

She regarded Rusty miserably as he mounted up with an effort. "What should I do?"

"I can't tell you that." He held the dancing bay in check and looked down at her with sage brown eyes. "But I can tell you this: Two wrongs don't make a right."

His piece said, Rusty reined his horse around and rode off to work the herd. Chronic arthritis or no, he had a job to do. And with Big Tom gone and both spring break and branding starting next week, it was up to him to continue teaching and shaping and molding Tony to take over the ranch someday.

But who better to show a boy the ropes than his own father? Especially if that father had won All-Around Cowboy honors three years running at the Circle C's annual Fourth of July barbecue and rodeo?

After a moment of mental lip-biting Jeannie spun on her heel and headed toward the house. She had to see Rafe. Today. What Big Tom had done to them was wrong. Now it was up to her to do the right thing.

"May I help you?"

"Rafe Martinez, please."

"Mr. Martinez is with a client right now."

The secretary had a Spanish accent that seemed to purr and a square face that might have been lifted from one of the friezes at Chichen Itza.

Jeannie realized she should have called first, instead of just changing her clothes, catching her hair back in a banana clip, and jumping into her car for an impetuous visit. But she hated to think she'd come all this way for nothing.

"Are you sure he couldn't spare me a couple of minutes?" She let a note of urgency creep into her voice.

"Let me see if he can squeeze you in," the secretary said, adjusting her black horn-rimmed glasses.

But after consulting the appointment calendar on her desk, the dark-haired woman shook her head regretfully. "He has a luncheon meeting with his campaign manager in half an hour, followed by a court appearance this afternoon." She turned the page and said with brisk efficiency, "However, I would be glad to make an appointment for you tomorrow"—now she glanced up inquiringly—"Ms. . . . ?"

"Crane. Jeannie Crane."

As if it had come unhinged, the secretary's jaw dropped when the significance of Jeannie's name sank in. She had obviously typed the letter that Rafe had sent via special delivery, which meant she knew the reason for the surprise visit.

Jeannie felt a blistering flush burst into

flame upon her cheeks, but from years of habit she squared her shoulders and lifted her chin to a determined angle. "Shall I wait?"

"Of course Ms. Crane." The secretary, having recovered from her initial shock, indicated the grouping of sofa and chairs. "Would you like some coffee?"

"No, thank you." Jeannie crossed to an armchair and sat down. She hated to place herself at a disadvantage by dealing with Rafe where his word was law, but Tony's future happiness depended on his parents putting the past behind them and settling this out of court.

The secretary resumed typing, her fingers flying over the keys. Their castanetlike cadence played counterpoint to the accordion-based *conjunto* music coming from the radio on her desk.

Rafe had remained true to his roots by hanging his shingle on the west side of San Antonio, where the majority of the Hispanic population lived and worked and played. Jeannie had experienced a whole host of emotions as she'd driven along the streets, remembering that long-ago day she'd come looking for Rafe to tell him she was pregnant. Then the vast barrio had seemed like an alien nation; now it almost felt like home.

After parking her Ford Explorer at the only available meter, Jeannie had found herself behaving as if she belonged. During the walk down the long block to the two-story brick building that housed Rafe's law office, she'd paused to window-shop when a pretty shawl in a small neighborhood store caught her eye. She'd smiled and said *"Buenas dias"* to two old men conducting a bull session in rapid-fire Spanish on the sidewalk. She'd frowned with maternal pique when a gang of teenagers who looked as if they should have been in school cruised by in a rolling boombox of a car.

Once inside the office, she'd been suitably impressed by the subtle south-of-the border ambiance. Hanging plants and huge trees rooted in whitewashed pots curtained the plate-glass window. Comfortable furniture in neutral colors and a handloomed cotton rug in the varying shades of the desert sand provided the perfect setting for a museum-quality collection of Mexican pottery and the vivid Diego Rivera prints that adorned the walls. Current issues of *Texas Monthly* and *Ombre* sat side-by-side on a tiered stone cock-tail table.

She cooled her heels for what seemed an eternity, though in reality she only waited about fifteen minutes before the door to Rafe's private office opened. He emerged in the company of a man, portly and mustached, who sounded terribly grateful that Rafe had agreed to represent him in traffic court.

Jeannie's heartbeat sped up at the sight of

Rafe, who hadn't seen her yet. Wearing a sedate gray suit, a striped shirt, and a retro necktie that pulled it all together, he looked sensational. His dark head was bent at a listening angle; his blue eyes were crinkled at the corners; his silver earring seemed totally in keeping with the flavor of his surroundings.

Fiddling nervously with one of the gold hoops in her own ears, she waited for him to finish his conversation with his client. The butterflies in her stomach had a heyday as the two men shook hands in farewell, and she decided that she'd made a terrible mistake showing up unannounced like this. He might reject her idea out of hand. Might laugh in her face. He might even kick—

"I'd be glad to sign a promissory note for my fee." The client's statement snapped Jeannie out of her worried daze.

Rafe dropped his hand and gave a dismissive shrug. "If a man's handshake is no good, neither is his signature."

After the door closed behind the departing client, the secretary announced, "There's someone else to see you, Mr. Martinez."

Rafe's eyes blazed like blue neon when he looked in Jeannie's direction. "What are you doing here?"

She stood, resisting the nervous urge to smooth her bleached denim skirt. "We need to talk."

"It's a little late for that, isn't it?" he remarked caustically.

"It's never too late where Tony's concerned," she returned calmly.

When he didn't immediately dispute her declaration, she bent down to pick up her purse, treating him to a glimpse of smooth white thigh. And when she straightened, her breasts thrust proudly against the red cotton tank top she'd tucked into her skirt.

Desire flared deep in Rafe's belly as she started toward him. She had that same walk—head high, shoulders squared. She looked so comfortable in her own skin that it made a man want to crawl inside her and never come out. But her betrayal still burned inside Rafe, laying waste to passion and leaving resentment in its wake.

Jeannie came to a halt within an arm's reach of him. A torrent of love and regret spilled through her as she looked up into his familiar, handsome face and met his challenging stare. His cold reception might have intimidated a lesser woman, but this woman had come too far to back down now.

"May we talk in private?" she asked politely.

"By all means," he agreed with a trace of mockery.

Rafe told his secretary to hold his calls before grudgingly ushering Jeannie into his office and closing the door. Setting one hip and thigh on the edge of his black marble desktop, he crossed his arms over that muscular chest and said cuttingly, "So, talk."

Jeannie's temper skyrocketed. How dare he be so rude as to fail to even offer her a chair? Not that she would have taken it. She was too nervous to sit. But he wasn't the only one who'd been manipulated by Big Tom. And this was their son's future she'd come to discuss.

On that thought she swallowed her anger and spoke in a civil tone. "I got your letter this morning."

His eyes were as expressionless as flat blue stones. "I assume I'll be hearing from your attorney soon."

"No."

"Oh?"

"I'm not going to fight you on this."

He raised a skeptical brow—this was Big Tom's daughter he was dealing with, after all. "Why the sudden change of heart?"

"I don't want to hurt Tony." She answered so emphatically, he had to give her the benefit of the doubt.

"Did he ask about me?"

"Yes."

His cynical guise crumbled, and a spasm of hope crossed his face. "What did you tell him?"

"That you were a friend of Big Tom's." She saw he was about to voice an objection and rushed to stall him. "I thought you should spend some time together, get acquainted with each other, before we break the news that you're his father."

He tried her idea on for size and found it suited him fine. "Where? When?"

"The lawyer in you is beginning to show." Despite her exasperated tone, the glimmer in her gray eyes told him she was only teasing.

"Everybody's got their faults," he replied with dry aplomb.

They shared a smile, the first in eleven years, and it felt wonderful on both sides.

"I take it you have a plan for getting the two of us together?" he prompted then.

She nodded, remembering the agenda his secretary had reeled off. "I know you're busy, so I'll try to make this fast."

He shook his head and reached behind him to press the buzzer on the intercom. "Nothing is more important to me than deciding the future of our son."

Our son. Her heart swelled at his declaration, for she'd despaired of ever hearing it.

When instructed to cancel his lunch for today and reschedule it for tomorrow, his secretary asked, "And what should I tell Mr. Quinones if he wants to know why the change in plans?"

Rafe's eyes met Jeannie's with a promise that made her entire body pulse. "Tell him I've got some family business to take care of."

Six

"Do you realize this is the first time we've ever gone anywhere together in broad daylight?"

Jeannie felt a sharp stab of pain at Rafe's pointed question. Their fragile truce was broken, through no fault of hers. Perturbed, she set her iced tea down and wondered how she'd gotten herself into this predicament.

They had left his law office and walked around the corner to a small Mexican restaurant that he frequently patronized. The proprietors, a middle-aged couple who were not only clients but also ardent political supporters of his, had greeted them effusively and given them a corner table where they could talk in private. The waitress had taken their orders, then left them to their own devices.

Now, with Rafe demanding an answer to his

opening question and Jeannie determined not to dredge up old regrets, she sighed theatrically and said, "How quickly they forget."

He frowned. "Forget what?"

"The county fair."

"Ah, yes, I remember it well." His enlightened gaze moved from her sun-kissed hair to her silvery eyes. Then a grin lifted one corner of his brooding lips. "You and Olivia were fourteen-year-old brats—"

"I was fourteen; she was thirteen."

"But brats nonetheless."

"Neither one of us could drive yet, so we talked you into taking us—"

"You *hounded* me into taking you." Now it was his turn to correct her.

"We asked you to try and win—"

"You *begged* me to throw baseballs at milk bottles."

"You won her a stuffed frog and me a teddy bear," she reminded him softly.

"She gave the frog to Enrique, who promptly tore it to shreds." But his voice was gently gruff.

"Tony slept with my teddy bear until he was three."

Rafe saw the startled look in her eyes and knew that her revelation had surprised her as much as it did him.

Jeannie looked away evasively, realizing too late that she'd just told him too much.

"Be careful now, these are really hot," the waitress warned, relieving the telling silence that had suddenly fallen between them. She set sizzling platters of chile rellenos, served with beans and rice, in front of them. Then she refilled Jeannie's glass and brought Rafe his beer before going to wait on another customer.

"Mmmm . . ." Grateful for an excuse to change the subject, Jeannie picked up her fork and dug into the cheese-stuffed peppers. "These look delicious."

Rafe ignored his food. "I wonder how Big Tom would feel about our sitting at the same table?"

He was referring to her father's rule that the help—in this instance the Martinez family—eat in their unit of the fourplex rather than at the main house. That meant Maria either had to cook two separate meals, one for the Cranes and one for her husband and children, or she had to cart leftovers home and reheat them.

With composure she swallowed a bite, took another sip of tea, then blotted her lips with a paper napkin before she looked at him. "I had nothing to do with that."

"Rusty always ate with you."

"Rusty had no one to cook for him."

His lips twisted wryly. "And Rusty's an Anglo."

Jeannie dropped her gaze, at a loss for words. Rafe's fingers—long and bronzed, with wispy black hair at the base—slid up and down the bottle where condensation had made it slippery, and a thrill that had nothing to do with the spicy food rose up from her stomach.

Because her reaction annoyed her, she took it out on him, setting her fork down and demanding irritably, "Why do you keep doing that?"

"Doing what?"

"Throwing the past in my face."

"It feels good." Boldly and without apology, his blue eyes drifted down to the front of her tank top. As though he'd touched them, as if they remembered the feathery caress of his fingertips, her breasts began to bead against the soft cotton.

Resenting the fact that he still possessed the power to arouse her, she folded her arms across her chest. "So if it feels good, do it?"

He lifted his gaze to her face. "You've got it."

She looked down at the table again, her stomach taking another roller-coaster ride when he skimmed a drop of moisture off the beer bottle and rubbed it between his thumb and forefinger.

Jeannie watched, mesmerized by that lazy circling motion before she realized that Rafe was doing it on purpose. Then she balled her hands into fists on her lap and met his knowing blue eyes. Not for the world would she admit defeat.

"I thought we came here to discuss getting you and Tony together," she said with a touch of asperity.

"We did," he acknowledged tightly. "But before we make any plans for the future, I've got to catch up on the past."

She shook her head, puzzled. "I don't understand."

"Big Tom hated me." Rafe's lips formed a thin, bitter line. "So what I want to know is, what did he say when you told him you were pregnant with my child?"

Jeannie groped around for an easy way to say it, but there wasn't one. "He wanted me to have an abortion."

From across the table she sensed his reaction. His body got tense. His face grew as chilly as the polar ice cap. She saw him push his plate aside and followed suit, her appetite vanishing in view of his anguish.

"Obviously you refused," he said tonelessly.

"I told him it was too late, that I was too far along."

"What did he say then?"

"That if I didn't go to a home for unwed mothers and put my baby up for adoption, he would disown me."

His jaw hardened at the idea of her own father emotionally blackmailing her like that. "And instead you went . . . where?"

"To Houston." She heaved a sigh tinged with yesterday's tears. "I stayed with my aunt—my mother's younger sister—until Tony was born."

Rafe's throat grew tight at the thought of all it had cost her to keep his child over Big Tom's strenuous objections. "What made him change his mind and let you come back to the ranch?" he asked her then.

"I think he finally realized he'd lost control over me, that he was going to be the loser this time around." Jeannie's eyes misted with maternal pride. "That, and the fact that Tony was the most beautiful baby ever born."

"An unbiased viewpoint of course."

She laughed. "But of course."

"He looks like me," he said, sobering.

"The mirror image."

"And how did Big Tom feel about looking into my face every morning, noon, and night for ten years?" The timbre of his voice expressed a very real concern.

"I never asked him." Jeannie chose her words with caution, not wanting to hurt him any more than she had to. "But frankly I think he saw Tony as an extension of himself. His grandson. A Crane, not a Martinez."

"So he didn't hold his Hispanic blood against him?"

"If he had, I'd have been gone just like this." She snapped her fingers, demonstrating dramatically. "He knew it too."

Rafe relaxed his rigid posture and reached across the table, taking her slender hand in his. He couldn't imagine all she'd been through because of him, not even when he could see it reflected so clearly in her eyes. The hell of being estranged from her father and bearing a baby alone made his own rocky road to success seem like the highway to heaven.

Jeannie sealed her lips together to keep from sighing with ecstasy when he turned her hand over and placed a kiss in the center of her palm. His lips were as soft as a sable brush against her sensitive skin. The warmth of his breath sent threads of heat spiraling along her arm. His words, when they came, were music to her soul.

"That's for giving life to my son," he murmured.

"*Our* son," she stressed softly.

"Our son," he agreed, meeting her eyes across the table.

The hot, oily aroma of their unfinished food wafted under their noses. Someone dropped a glass, causing a crash and a string of curses to fill the air. The door opened for new customers and closed on old ones. Spanish greetings mingled with English good-byes, bespeaking the gradual merging of two proud cultures.

For all that Rafe and Jeannie noticed, they might have been alone in a moonlit meadow again, making plans for their future as if they really had one.

"Was there something wrong with the food?" the waitress asked, breaking the spell that had fallen over her bedazzled customers.

"No." Jeannie pulled her hand free and glanced at the anxiously hovering girl. "Why?"

"You've hardly touched your lunch."

"It's my fault." Rafe shouldered the blame with a smile. "I grabbed her fork hand and forced her to follow me on a stroll down memory lane."

"Speaking of which . . ." Jeannie said when

the waitress had cleared away their plates but left their drinks and lunch check. "Where did you all go when you left the ranch?"

"The Rio Grande Valley."

She sipped her tea and tasted regret. "No wonder I couldn't find you."

"My parents picked the last of the summer vegetables, then grapefruit and oranges that winter," he remembered aloud. "And Olivia and Enrique went to school in a tin shack that had been set up for migrant workers' kids."

"What did you do?" she asked around the lump that had formed in her throat at the thought of what his family had endured as a result of Big Tom's bigotry.

His expression betrayed none of the bitterness welling inside him. "Picked tomatoes and peppers for a couple of weeks, until I had enough money to call you and tell you I was coming back for you. Then I told my parents to go get their green cards, kissed Olivia and Enrique good-bye, and headed for the nearest pay phone."

She knew what was coming next and quickly lowered her lashes to veil her tear-filled eyes. To think that something as simple as a phone call had caused so many complications . . .

"After hearing you'd eloped," he continued in a raspy voice, "I picked fruit for the rest of that season, then enrolled in law school the following semester."

She lifted her gaze back to him, questioning

something he'd mentioned earlier. "Did your parents ever get their green cards?"

"Better than that—they got their citizenship papers."

"That's wonderful!"

His smile held all the pride and the promise of the red, white, and blue. "My father flies the flag every day that it doesn't rain, and my mother fixes a Fourth of July barbecue to rival the Circle C's."

She was pleased for the migrant couple but more concerned with their son's progress. "Law school is so expensive."

He grimaced. "Tell me about it."

"How did you manage to pay your tuition?"

"I did construction work the first two years, then clerked for a judge the third."

She could just picture him hustling from the classroom to the job site to moot court. "When did you find time to study?"

"I burned a lot of midnight oil."

"It must have been exhausting."

"But worth it, in the end."

"How were your grades?"

"Mostly A's." Rafe couldn't resist boasting a bit. "And I was editor of the law review my senior year."

Jeannie was duly impressed. "With that kind of record, I'm surprised some big law firm didn't snap you up straight out of school."

"I was invited to join several firms, but I was just too much of a maverick to fit their mold."

"And?" she asked, sensing there was more.

He gave her a mirthless smile. "And I wasn't interested in being their token minority."

"Not even for the money?"

"I've done all right for myself."

She toasted the visible signs of his success with her tea. "Here's to tailor-made suits and silk ties."

"Beats those hand-me-downs I lived in as a boy." He finished his beer but kept the bottle. "Let's go."

"You collect empties now?" she asked as she picked up her purse.

"I need it for court," he answered enigmatically, laying enough change atop the generous tip to cover the deposit charge.

Jeannie didn't get a chance to pursue that because, just as she stepped outside, she stumbled over a small crack in the concrete sidewalk. Rafe caught her, the tapered strength of his fingers encircling her arm and stirring embers that were better left banked.

"My knight in shining armor," she said with a smile.

"Surely you *joust*," he returned as he released her.

They shared a laugh and started walking in the direction of his office. But that brief contact left a residue of awareness that she tried to put from her mind as diligently as she tried to match his stride.

The delicate scent of roses wafting from a flower garden in front of a modest but well-maintained home had stiff competition from the pungent aroma of *yerba buena*—dried mint leaves—coming from someone else's open kitchen window.

"Do you live around here?" she asked as they turned the corner and approached his office.

He stopped and pointed skyward. "When I bought the building, I gutted it and converted the second floor into a loft."

"You live over the office?" She looked up and, sure enough, saw wooden blinds at the windows.

As she preceded him into the anteroom, he gave her golden plume of hair, cascading from that plastic clip, a playful tug. "Wanna go up and see my collection of empties?"

She whipped her head around, the laughing reply "Don't you mean etchings?" burbling to her lips. But the comeback perished in her throat under his penetrating stare.

The secretary had gone to lunch in their absence, so they had the office to themselves. Their eyes connected in the air-conditioned stillness, and they both remembered vividly what good use they would have made of time alone in years gone by.

But that was then and this was now. He had a preliminary hearing this afternoon, and she had to pick their son up from school in a couple of hours.

"It's getting late," she noted nervously.

He shot his cuff back and glanced down at his watch, his dark hair gleaming in the sunlight that found its way through the leafy green fronds draping the window. "It's twelve thirty."

"When do you have to be in court?"

"The hearing starts in thirty minutes."

She figured it would take him a good fifteen minutes to get there, given the noon-hour traffic rush and the never-ending street repairs, and another five to find a parking place.

"We can talk on the phone tonight, after Tony goes to bed," she offered since he was in a hurry.

"We'll talk after court," he decreed before disappearing into his office.

It took a second for that to sink in. When the full impact of his statement finally registered, she swore under her breath and bolted after him.

"What do you mean, *after* court?" she demanded, positioning herself in front of his desk and bracing both fists upon her hips.

"I mean you're going with me." He placed the empty beer bottle in his burnished leather briefcase.

"But I—"

"The hearing shouldn't take more than an hour."

"An hour!"

He shrugged. "Two at the most."

"I have to pick up Tony at three."

"Can't Rusty do that?"

"He's riding herd today."

"What about Martha?"

Jeannie's mouth turned downward in an attractive sulk. "Tony's expecting me."

"Tony's had you to himself for ten years." Rafe's entreating blue eyes only added to his appeal. "All I'm asking you for is one afternoon."

"Oh, all right." She feigned an irritated sigh, but actually her heart was pounding with anticipation at the idea of seeing him in action. Besides, she was dying to know what he was going to do with that bottle. "I'll have to call the ranch, though."

"You can use my phone." He picked up his briefcase and headed for the door.

"Shakespeare was right," Jeannie grumbled good-naturedly as she dialed the Circle C.

"But if we killed off all the lawyers," Rafe countered in that same vein, "who would run for political office?"

"Precisely my point!"

He laughed and closed the door behind him just as Webb Bishop answered the phone at the ranch on the second ring.

"W—Webb?"

"Hello, Jeannie."

She shook her head in confusion. "What are you doing out there in the middle of the day?"

"I had a couple of hours to kill between hospital rounds and office calls, so I thought

I'd swing by and see how you're getting along."

"I'm fine," she said a bit too quickly. "Just fine."

"Good . . ." He cleared his throat. "Good."

A telling silence hummed on the line.

She rushed to fill it. "I'm in San Antonio right now."

"So Martha said."

Jeannie pinched her eyes shut at the note of resignation in his voice. Tears burned behind her lids. But it was over between them. Over before it had really begun. And there was no sense in prolonging the agony for either of them.

"Is Martha there now?" she asked with false animation.

"She's up to her elbows in bread dough." Which explained why Webb had answered the phone. "But I'd be glad to give her a message before I go."

She passed along her instructions, then said in parting, "Thank you for all you've done for Big Tom and for Tony and . . . and for me."

A gentleman to the bitter end, he made a gracious exit. "Good-bye, Jeannie."

"Good-bye, Webb," she whispered before she hung up, wishing with all her heart that she didn't have to break his. The problem was—

The problem was, he wasn't Rafe.

Seven

The courtroom was as quiet as a church.

People walked softly and spoke in whispers. Sounds were magnified: the hum of the air conditioner, the ticking of the clock on the wall, the shuffling of papers at the lawyers' tables, the squeak of the heavy doors.

Even though she was sitting on a wooden bench that looked remarkably like a pew, Jeannie was well aware that she wasn't in church. Nor did she think that Rafe's client—his hair as wiry as steel wool and his skin the color of sorghum molasses—bore the slightest resemblance to a choirboy.

A bartender by trade, he had admitted to shooting a customer during an argument. He also claimed he'd done it in self-defense. But since there'd been no one else in the bar at the time of the altercation, it was his word against the victim's. And who would believe a man with the word *killer* tattooed on his left arm?

The victim, who had lived to tell the tale, looked like a candidate for Confirmation by comparison. His hair was neatly trimmed and combed, his face clean-shaven and hospital-pale. He wore a dark suit, a tasteful tie, and a sling on his right arm.

"All rise," the bailiff said in a sonorous tone.

Jeannie stood along with everyone else when the judge made his entrance. A man who looked to be in his mid-sixties, he wore a black robe and a pair of Ben Franklin glasses.

"Please be seated," he instructed everyone after he'd taken his place on the bench. Behind him an American flag and the flag of the state of Texas drooped on their stanchions. He nodded to the prosecuting attorney, then said, "You may proceed."

Jeannie had a front-row seat, which allowed her an unobstructed view of everyone and everything. She'd never been in court before, not even on a traffic charge, so she was anxious to learn how the system worked. Now she leaned forward a little, the better to hear.

On the drive to the courthouse Rafe had explained that during the hearing the prosecutor had to present enough evidence to convince the judge that the defendant—Rafe's client, in this case—should be bound over for trial on felony charges of assault with a deadly weapon. If Rafe could prove otherwise, through a combination of evidence and examination, the charges would be dropped and his client would go free.

The prosecutor called the arresting officer.

A burly man with close-cropped hair and bulldog jowls, the policeman took the stand and began to tell the court how he'd been called to the scene by a passerby and caught Rafe's client with smoking gun in hand.

As she listened to the prosecutor and the policeman driving nails into the defendant's coffin, Jeannie kept glancing at Rafe, who was sitting at the counsel table with an impassive expression. From the heavily starched cotton of his shirt collar to the hand-tooled toes of his eelskin boots, he looked like the Madison Avenue prototype of a prosperous Texas attorney. But there the resemblance ended.

No courtroom pallor lightened his skin and no desk jockey's paunch ballooned his stomach. His burnt-sienna coloring was due in large measure to his heritage, but his superb physical condition was strictly the result of the five miles he'd told her he jogged every morning.

His black hair was a trifle shorter in front than it had been the day of the funeral, though it was still collar-length at the back. The silver earring, which she had mistakenly assumed he would remove for the hearing, winked at her in the fluorescent lighting whenever he moved his head to make a note to himself during the policeman's testimony.

"Pass the witness," the prosecutor said when he was finished presenting this part of his case.

"Thank you." Rafe stood, tall and somehow invincible, seeming to dominate the courtroom through sheer determination.

As he picked up one of the photographs that the prosecutor had introduced into evidence and carried it toward the witness stand, Jeannie couldn't help but remember a passionate young man proclaiming that he wanted to become a lawyer because he wanted to make a difference. She had always believed in him. Always supported him. But until today she'd never really understood the terrible injustices that had spurred his lofty ambitions.

Born in the charity ward of a barrio hospital, he'd cut his teeth on grinding poverty and gang warfare. The oldest child of migrant workers, he'd learned to sleep cramped, to wear cast-offs, and to eat whatever was put in front of him and be grateful for it. A streetwise attorney, he knew from his own experiences that Justice occasionally lifted her blindfold to see what color a person was, how he dressed, where he lived, and who his friends were.

Rafe Martinez was a rebel with a cause, she

realized. A modern-day gladiator whose arena was a courtroom rather than a coliseum. And in most cases, he was his clients' last chance for a fair hearing.

"Officer," he said now, "I'm handing you this photograph of the scene of the shooting again and asking you to tell the court what that object on the floor to the right of the victim is."

"It's a beer bottle."

From the corner of her eye Jeannie saw the victim squirm in his chair and adjust his arm sling, as if he hadn't counted on having to sit through this line of questioning.

Then Rafe commanded her full attention again, standing relaxed and poised before the witness stand and asking, "What kind of beer bottle?"

"I don't know." The policeman squinted at the photograph, then shook his head. "I can't read the label."

A smile broke across Rafe's handsome face, briefly relieving it of its foreboding austerity. Jeannie's heart fluttered at the sight of his firm lips softening, his white teeth flashing, and the deep lines on either side of his mouth denting in.

"Let me rephrase that," he said then, the twinkle fleeing from his blue eyes and his expression turning solemn as he got back to the business at hand. "Does anything appear to be wrong with the beer bottle?"

Now the policeman nodded. "The bottom is broken off."

Utterly fascinated, Jeannie listened as Rafe went on to build his foundation, brick by brick, until he finally got to the point he really wanted the policeman to make.

"So, Officer, are you saying that a broken beer bottle can be used as a weapon to assault a person?"

"Yes, it can."

"And have you ever seen anyone stabbed or cut with a broken beer bottle?"

"Yes, I have."

"Have you ever seen anyone killed as a result of an attack with a broken beer bottle?"

"Objection—irrelevant."

"Overruled."

Rafe repeated the question.

"Yes, I have," the policeman answered.

"So, in your opinion can a broken beer bottle be used as a deadly weapon?"

"Objection—calls for a conclusion."

Rafe didn't stand still for it this time. He spun toward the judge, his eyes blazing with barely restrained fury. Jeannie expected him to spit nails when he spoke, but he surprised her by arguing both calmly and convincingly that the police officer had already been certified by the prosecutor as an expert in the field of what could and could not be used as a deadly weapon.

"Overruled." The judge nodded to the policeman. "You may answer."

"Yes, it can be used as a deadly weapon."

"Tell me, Officer," Rafe encouraged, "was the broken beer bottle in this photograph removed from the crime scene by the police investigative unit, and if so, where is it now?"

"We have it in our bag of evidence," the prosecutor answered in the policeman's stead.

Rafe took the broken beer bottle from the prosecutor and had it marked as Defendant's Exhibit 1. The way he handled it, loose and easy, his strong brown fingers coiled around the smooth glass neck so that the jagged bottom faced the floor, told Jeannie more than she'd ever wanted to know about how he'd managed to survive those early years on the streets. It just about killed her to think that at Tony's age, or younger, he'd literally fought for his life.

"Did your department fingerprint this bottle?" he asked the officer then.

"Yes, we did."

"And whose fingerprints did you find on it?"

"The victim's."

Once again, the man with the sling drew everyone's attention by shifting in his chair. All eyes turned to him just as his face fractured into something ugly and mean. Then he caught himself, smoothing his expression with the hand of his good arm.

Rafe reacted to his discomfort in dramatic

fashion, raising the bottle for the policeman's convenience and almost scaring the bejesus out of Jeannie as he asked in booming voice, "And where did you find the victim's fingerprints on this broken beer bottle?"

"We found a partial thumbprint on the body of the bottle," the officer said, pointing a cautious finger, "just above the place where it had been broken. And then we found a full series of prints on the neck."

After satisfying himself and the court that all the fingerprints matched the victim's, Rafe put the bottle on the evidence table, laying it on its side so that its vicious-looking bottom faced the judge's bench. Then he returned to the counsel table, opened the briefcase he'd left by his chair, reached in and removed a bottle that Jeannie recognized as the one he'd taken from the restaurant.

"With the court's indulgence," he said, holding the unbroken bottle aloft like some medieval standard of battle, "we would like to engage in a little demonstration."

The judge nodded. "The court has no objection."

Rafe approached the witness stand, his stride brisk and confident. Jeannie sat up straighter as he got down to the nitty-gritty.

"I don't want you to take the chance of cutting yourself, Officer," he said, "so I'm going to hand you an unbroken, empty beer bottle that is identical to the broken beer bottle that was retrieved at the scene of the shooting and that is now in evidence—"

"Objection!" The prosecutor leapt to his feet, seeming to realize—albeit belatedly—where this was leading. "This isn't show-and-tell."

Rafe turned back to the bench, smoldering with absolute authority. "Your Honor, all I want the officer to do is to demonstrate for the court at no risk to himself where exactly the victim's partial thumbprint was found on the body of the broken beer bottle."

Jeannie held her breath while the judge considered his request, then let it out in a relieved sigh when he said, "It's a little irregular, but I've already granted permission."

The prosecutor sat down with a disgusted *thump*.

Her mind abuzz, she watched as Rafe handed the beer bottle to the police officer and asked him to hold it in such a fashion that his thumb would be in the same place as the print that had been lifted off the bottle.

The officer did so, gripping it around the body as if he were going to take a drink from it. Rafe thanked him, took the unbroken bottle back, and returned it to his briefcase.

"Now," he said, taking the broken bottle off the evidence table and carrying it back to the witness stand, "I'm going to hand you this bottle, and I'm going to ask you to exercise extreme caution as you hold it by the neck, placing your thumb and four fingers in the same place as the prints that were lifted off it during the course of your investigation."

The prosecutor, face pink, shot to his feet again. "Objection—probative value."

Rafe's eyes turned stony, his voice steely. "Your Honor, the victim in this case has alleged that the defendant, after serving him several beers, refused to serve him anything more. The victim has also alleged that when he argued the matter, the defendant pulled a gun—a legally registered gun, I might add— out from behind the bar and shot him for no good reason.

"It is our contention—a contention we intend to prove during this preliminary hearing—that the defendant refused further service to the victim because the victim was loudly, rudely, obnoxiously, and dangerously drunk. We also intend to prove that when the defendant told the victim he had had enough to drink, the victim smashed the bottle he had just emptied against the edge of the bar and came after the defendant with the intention of going for the jugular.

"Furthermore we intend to prove through examination and through a preponderance of the evidence that the alleged victim in this case is actually a victimizer, that he has a history of violent behavior toward others when he's drinking, and that the defendant, when faced with that broken beer bottle, had no recourse but to shoot the victim in self-defense.

"In summary, Your Honor, we want to show through this exhibition that this *victim*"—Rafe stressed the word mockingly as he glared at the man wearing the sling with the full candle-power of his moral disapproval—"triggered his own tragedy."

The prosecutor renewed his objection, adding snidely, "An 'exhibition' of this sort could only be called inflammatory."

"Overruled," the judge said. "I want to see what the defendant was faced with."

Rafe turned back toward the witness stand and moved in for the kill. "Officer, would you please show the court where the victim's fingerprints were found on the neck of this bottle?"

Jeannie shivered, realizing what a sheltered life she'd led when the policeman wrapped his fingers around the neck of the bottle, picked it up, and held the broken end of it out in front of him. And seeing the judge wince and rear back slightly when the policeman swung that jagged maw in his direction, slashing the air between the witness stand and the bench, she also realized that Rafe had made his point about the bottle's potential as a lethal weapon in the most effective manner possible.

"No further questions," Rafe said as he relieved the officer of the broken beer bottle, replaced it on the evidence table, and resumed his seat with a triumphant smile.

Eight

"You love it, don't you?"

"What—winning?"

Jeannie smiled as Rafe sped under the freeway overpass, following Commerce Street as it led into the heart of the West Side. They'd just left the hearing, which had lasted a little over an hour. When all was said and done, the charges had been dropped and his client had walked out of court a free man. Now it was back to his office for him and, as soon as they decided how to get him and Tony together, back to Bolero for her.

The windows were down, and Jeannie's senses were assaulted by the sights and sounds and smells of Rafe's home ground. A cluster of people in their gimme caps and work shirts sat fanning themselves on a wooden bench, waiting patiently for the bus. A guitar player stood in front of a souvenir shop, strumming up tourist business with melodies of Old Mexico and new merchandise. An open church door emitted the faint aroma of funeral incense.

"I'm sure you love winning," she said as the building where he lived and worked came into view, "but I was talking about the practice of the law."

He turned into the side lot and nosed the Corvette into his parking space. "Win or lose, I've always enjoyed a good fight."

Jeannie started to laugh, then stopped as a memory crept in, one she had almost forgotten. Rafe, returning to the ranch after running into Bolero to pick up some cattle feed, his face bruised and his knuckles bleeding. She'd known without being told that someone had either called him a terrible name or simply called him on his right to be there, and that he'd struck back. Her heart had ached for him, as if she'd been attacked as well, but he hadn't wanted her sympathy.

"Well, you were wonderful in that courtroom today," she said in all sincerity.

He gave a self-effacing shrug and killed the engine. "Just doing my part to keep the system honest."

"You know what really burns me about the system?"

"What?"

"When a judge releases someone who's obviously guilty—a confessed criminal, for instance—on a technicality."

"For your information, judges don't make the laws. Or the loopholes either. So it's your state senator and your representative—"

Jeannie laughed and held up her hands in surrender. "I sense a political speech coming."

Rafe chuckled. "Point taken."

She tucked her sandaled foot under the opposite thigh and turned in the low-slung seat. Her denim skirt modestly covered her knees, but her thin bra and tank top did nothing to hide the shape of her firm breasts. "Seriously now, what made you think to check and see whether the victim in this case had a record?"

"*Alleged* victim." He squared around in his seat to face her and crooked an elbow on the wheel, causing his suitcoat to fall open. Red silk suspenders added a touch of pizzazz to his high-powered appearance, and the platinum face of his watch peeked out from beneath his shirt cuff.

Jeannie ceded his point with a nod, remembering now how surprised she'd been when, with the *alleged* victim on the stand and sworn to tell the truth, Rafe had produced a rap sheet as long as her arm detailing other instances of violent behavior on his part.

As it had turned out, he'd even served a jail term for attacking someone else with a broken beer bottle. That information, coupled with the policeman's demonstration and the defendant's testimony, had convinced the judge that it was a cut-and-dried case of self-defense.

"You still haven't answered my question," she reminded him.

A slow smile teased the corners of his blue eyes. "Would you believe it was a lucky guess?"

She wrinkled her nose at him. "I'd say it was more like good detective work."

"Goes with the territory," he said with a verbal shrug.

"It also goes to show you how deceiving appearances can be," she declared.

A pair of creases formed between his eyebrows. "Because my client was black?"

Both her back and her voice stiffened. "Give me a break, will you?"

His slumberous eyes locked with hers across the console before lowering to her mouth. "I'd rather give you a kiss."

Jeannie's pulse kicked into overdrive at Rafe's sensually gruff statement and right-of-possession gaze. She studied his face, sculptured in bronze, forced to admit that in spite of everything she wanted his kiss, wanted him.

Still, she shook her head, trying to apply the brakes to her racing heart, hoping to slow the momentum of her rushing blood. Until three days ago their lovemaking had been a memory gilded by time and distance and a wonderful boy named Tony. Now it felt as if she were careening toward the sheer cliffs of those youthful transgressions again.

"What is it they say?" he asked huskily, reaching over to tug on a wisp of silky blond hair that had escaped its banana clip confines to curl upon her cheek. "To the victor belong the spoils."

Instinct warned her to back up before he moved to kiss her, but as the door handle poking at her spine pointedly reminded her, there was no place to go.

Except forward . . .

She felt herself being inexorably drawn to him and dragged air into her lungs to tell him that too much water had passed under the bridge. But when he cupped her face between his lean brown hands and let the warm mist of his breath caress his lips, she found herself drowning in the treacherous sea of today's desire.

"Jeannie . . . Jeannie," he murmured, her name on his lips blotting out the loss of time, the river of tears, the years of torment.

His scent filled her nostrils—musky, mixed with the woody essence of his aftershave and the starchy smell of his shirt. Her eyes drifted closed as his lips glided over hers, rubbing her mouth softly, repeatedly, seductively, until her lips parted of their own volition.

"Rafe . . ." she whispered against his hungering mouth, welcoming him home at long last.

He took his time, teasing and tasting, sampling and savoring, whetting her appetite for more. She wrapped her hands around his neck and drew his head down, demanding all of him. He deepened the kiss, the liquid fire of his tongue igniting heat waves that spread like velvet ripples inside her chest.

The Corvette enclosed them in a cocoon of preserved leather and passion renewed, but the console prevented them from making the reunion complete. Just as they had so many times in that ancient Studebaker, though, they made do.

Rafe flattened one hand on the center of her back and let it coast down to the sensitive shallows of her spine. His other hand rode up the delicate birdcage of her ribs to the outer curve of her breast, reshaping the soft mound of flesh to fit his palm, rediscovering the hard pearl at its peak.

Jeannie gave a start as his flicking thumb set off electric sparks inside her. She reveled in the feeling, exploring the back of his neck, tunneling her fingers through his hair, reacquainting herself with that virile thickness, that springy texture. Tentatively then, because this was a new experience for her, she touched his earring.

They had always communicated well on a sexual level. Once he'd reached over and playfully pinched her nipple, and she'd slapped his hand away with a pained "Ouch!" Another time she'd run her nails lightly up the inside of his thigh, and he'd laid back in the spring grass with a pleasured "Ahhh." Now, much to their mutual delight, they found the lines were still wide open.

Emboldened by his low growl of approval, she fondled his silver earring, turning it, toying with it, warming it to her touch. Encouraged by the tremulous, catchy sound she made in her throat, he fed his hunger for her with tender love bites, nipping his way down her neck, lipping his way back up, leaving her trembling in his tongue's wake.

"This is crazy," she scolded in a strangled voice. "Making out like teenagers in a car."

His answering laugh warmed the hollow of her ear. "Ah, but think how much we've learned since then."

Rafe's huskily spoken remark stung Jeannie like a whiplash, reminding her that while he had probably learned all kinds of things in the last eleven years, the full extent of her knowledge was limited to him.

Her hands dropped to his shoulders; her fingers dug in. "I have to go."

"Stay in town tonight." He drew away, just far enough to be able to take her face into both hands.

"I can't." She shook her head, denying him. Denying herself in the process.

He kissed the throbbing pulse at her temple. "We'll have dinner on the Riverwalk—"

She cut him off at the pass. "Tony will be home from school in a little—"

"And then later—"

"You'll show me your collection of empties?"

"I'll show you mine if you'll show me yours."

"You've seen mine," she said in a constricted voice.

He nuzzled her cheek and the corner of an eye, sending shivers along her skin. "Not lately."

"And not now," came her sharp reply.

Rafe got the message then, loud and clear. He let her go and laid his head back against the leather seat, staring out the windshield at the solid brick wall in front of them as if it were the most fascinating thing he'd ever seen.

"We did it all backward, didn't we?" He rolled his head her way, the regret in his blue velvet eyes echoing in his voice as he answered his own question. "Made a baby before we ever even had a real date."

Jeannie breathed in but couldn't breathe out past the tight little pain in her throat. She swallowed and looked down at her lap, blinking back the tears that threatened to spill.

"I wanted to take you places—to the movies, to the Dairy Queen, to your senior prom." He chuckled bitterly. "But good little Anglo girls didn't go out with big, bad greasers. So instead I took you to the backseat of my car."

"You took me into your arms." She reached over and smoothed his wind-rumpled hair back from his forehead, erasing his pained frown with her tender ministrations. "And that was the only place on earth I wanted to be."

Rafe captured her hand, linking their fingers over the console. "Believe me when I say I never meant to hurt you."

Jeannie looked down at their joined hands. "Nor I, you."

"If I'd known then what I know now, I wouldn't have let it happen."

"It wasn't *all* your fault."

"But I was older. I could have controlled things if I'd tried."

"And I could have said no if I'd wanted to."

He squeezed her hand. "Too bad we can't go back and start over."

She saw her opening and jumped in with both feet. "Maybe we can."

That got his attention. "Oh, yeah?"

"Yeah."

"How?"

"Walk me back to my car, and I'll tell you how."

He grinned. "You drive a hard bargain."

"Don't I, though?" she agreed saucily.

Rafe rubbed Jeannie's knuckle with his thumb, wondering how she would react if, instead, he just scooped her into his arms, carried her upstairs to the loft over his office and took her straight to his bed.

For eleven years she'd been off-limits, forbidden to him first by her father and then by his own innate respect for the marriage vows he'd been led to believe she had taken. Now he wanted to make up for lost time.

He wanted to touch her again. See his hands on her ivory skin, feel her naked and quivering with need beneath his questing fingers, trail fire paths along her breasts, her ribs, her belly, and lower. He wanted to taste her again. Sip at the taut sweetness of her nipples, feast on the banquet of her femininity, lap at the honey of her. He wanted to make love to her again. Bury his face in the curve of her shoulder, his body in her creamy warmth, and take her all the places he'd never taken her before.

But what he wanted to do and what he did were two different things. He released her hand, one slender finger at a time, and said, "Deal."

Jeannie experienced a small pang of regret as she reached down to pick up her purse. For a moment there she'd thought she'd detected that old flame burning in Rafe's blue eyes. The one that had always ignited a torch in her. But when he got out on the driver's side and came around to open the passenger door, the fire was gone and only the remembered glow of friendship remained.

Hand in hand, the feeling so natural that neither of them stopped to think that this was how it had all started between them, they left his Corvette behind and headed for her car.

"So," he said, "what's this grand scheme of yours for getting Tony and me together?"

"As you may remember," she began, "spring break and branding always start at the same time."

He remembered, all right. Remembered that he'd busted his butt for Big Tom while the rest of his college class had busted kegs in Palm Beach or on Padre Island.

Other memories, better ones, canceled out the bitter. He remembered gray eyes and a rancher's daughter, her jeans skin-tight and her leather jacket gaping open to reveal a snip of white lace camisole that made warm, moist air climb down his chest. Remembered, too, that he'd gone back to school with more dreams in his head than dollars in hand.

"They start pretty soon, don't they?"

"Next week."

He was one step ahead of her now. "And you want me to come out to the ranch and work with—"

"You wouldn't have to work," she hastened to assure him. "I just thought you might want to get acquainted with Tony on his own turf."

"How's he going to feel about some stranger—"

"You're an old friend, remember?"

He smiled ruefully and rolled his eyes as if to say, "Get serious."

She gave him a gentle, none-of-that-now nudge in the ribs. "Tony's nothing like Big Tom—"

"Thank God for small favors."

"He loves company," she continued earnestly. "And I just know he'll love you too."

Rafe found himself breathing easier at the news. For some time now he'd been aware of a growing sense of dissatisfaction. He couldn't put his finger on it exactly, but it felt as if the walls were closing in on him. Part of it was the weather, the way the spring air just breathed of life renewed. And part of it was the dawning realization that the trappings of success were, to some degree, simply traps with solid-gold teeth.

Jeannie had been only partially right when she'd said he loved the practice of the law. What he really loved was the promise of the law. Truth and justice were admirable goals, but trying to right all the wrongs within the system was beginning to take its toll. He was frustrated because it was such a slow process. And when things bogged down, as they often did, he had to wonder if he wasn't tilting at the proverbial windmill.

Running helped, but that restlessness

stayed with him as he pounded the inner-city streets. It was a crazy in-the-craw feeling of being incomplete, of having nothing to show personally for all he'd accomplished professionally. And now that he'd found the missing links, his son and the mother of his son, he would do everything in his power to keep from losing them.

"What if I want to work?" Rafe asked now, the thought of saddling up and riding with Jeannie and Tony dulling some of the resentment he felt toward Big Tom.

"We can always use another hand." Jeannie smiled. The idea of seeing Rafe and Tony together at long last, of the three of them living and working and laughing just like the real family she'd dreamed about so long ago lifted her heart to a new high.

He told himself that it was none of his damn business, that she was free to see anyone she wanted to, but he was driven to ask, "What about Webb Bishop?"

"We're friends." At least she hoped they still were.

One down, and one to go.

She looked up at him inquiringly then, turnabout being fair play. "What about you?"

"Nobody recently—and never anybody as special as you."

For a moment neither of them said anything more.

"Is it going to be hard for you to get away on such short notice?" she asked finally.

"Monday shouldn't be much of a problem, but I'll have to check my calendar—"

"You could come on Sunday then and—"

"Commute the rest of the week if I have to."

Jeannie squeezed his hand, hard. "You'll do it?"

Rafe returned the pressure. "Try and stop me."

When they got to her car, they found that her meter had expired over an hour ago. They also found a parking ticket under the wiper blade.

"Thank heavens I know a good lawyer," she said, handing the ticket to him.

He tucked it into his jacket pocket, then backed her up against the hood, his eyes gleaming with laughter. "Are you sure you can afford my fee?"

Between the hot metal behind her and the hard male against her belly, Jeannie was stuck. And happily so. As she lifted her face to smile back at him, all the grief and the heartache of the last eleven years dissolved like mist under the warmth of the sun. She knew then that she loved him. That she'd never stopped loving him. She knew, too, that she would stay in town tonight if he would only ask her again.

She tilted her head in age-old invitation and answered his challenge with a throaty, "If I can't afford it, I'm sure we can work something out."

Rafe stepped back, reading between the lines but determined to do it right this time around. He wanted to make love to her. Long, slow, drive-her-out-of-her-mind love. But he didn't want her watching the clock, worrying about getting home to Tony the way she used to worry about getting back to the house before Big Tom discovered she was gone. And he knew now that what he felt for her would keep.

"Up you go." He opened the car door and gave her a hand as she climbed in.

She rolled the window down to say good-bye and saw the troubled expression he wore. "What's the matter?"

"I just realized I don't even know my son's full name."

"Anthony Thomas."

Rafe's heart spread like an eagle's wings within his chest. "Anthony for my father?"

Jeannie nodded, sensing and sharing his soaring jubilation. "And Thomas for mine."

A barrio church bell began ringing the three-o'clock Angelus, heralding her next revelation.

"I had Tony baptized in Houston," she said softly.

To put it mildly, he was stunned. "But you're not a Catholic."

"Oh, yes, I am."

"Since when?"

Her eyes warmed to his. "Since I took instructions while I was staying with my aunt."

Caution wagged a finger in the face of Rafe's joy. "And how did Tom the Baptist react to that?"

Jeannie was tempted to tell him that he'd sounded just like Big Tom then, but she hated to end such a promising day on such a sour note. "All that matters now is how much he loved Tony."

He smiled in grim resignation. "You're right."

"See you Sunday," she said, as she turned the key in the ignition.

Rafe delayed her departure by cupping her neck and drawing her head through the window, claiming her mouth in a kiss that made her heart dance a fandango. Jeannie's hand crept up to cradle his jaw, her fingers detaining him in return.

The church bell chimed its last when he finally drew back with a whispered. "*Vaya con Dios.*"

Nine

"If you were such a good friend of Grandpa's, how come you never came to see him when he was sick?"

Not the sort of greeting he'd expected from his own son, Rafe thought ruefully as he carried the saddle he'd brought to Bolero with him into the barn. And definitely not a good way to start the week. Still, it was a fair question and it deserved an honest answer.

First, though, he set his saddle, horn down, on the floor. Then he straightened and looked at Tony, who had followed him into the barn but had stopped just short of stepping into the empty stall where Jeannie had suggested he store his riding gear. And finally he gave that tough little cuss the answer he was waiting for. "Because nobody told me Big Tom was sick."

"You could've called." The boy's blue eyes studied him with open defiance, and his jaw was set in a small, rebellious line that the man recognized only too well.

Rafe raked an impatient hand through his hair, wondering where he should go from there. No sooner had he parked his car in front of the barn and begun unloading the truck when Tony had come up from behind and thrown down that gauntlet about his grandfather.

Anger flared in him as the realization that Big Tom had given him one of the most contemptuous Judas kisses since the Last Supper. Without stopping to think who he was really hurting, and with the distinct advantage of a ten-year head start, he'd turned Rafe's own flesh and blood against him.

It was a bitter pill, and one that didn't go down easily. But it was either swallow hard or spew the same kind of poison at his son that the narrow-minded rancher had.

Rafe's throat convulsed, yet he managed to say calmly, "I'm sorry now that I didn't call."

"You should be," Tony declared before rounding on his boot heel and heading for the barn's sliding door. He paused there and turned back, firing his parting volley in a high, pained voice that carried clearly along the concrete passageway connecting the stalls. "Grandpa was really lonesome for his friends before he died."

Rafe seriously considered going after Tony

and telling him exactly why Big Tom had spent his last days on earth with no one but his daughter and his grandson to comfort him. Outside of giving him the momentary satisfaction of striking back, though, the only purpose that would serve was to put him on Big Tom's level. And he had no intention of sinking that low.

There was something about Tony's defiant expression that hit him where he lived, he acknowledged as he went back out to the car to get his saddle blanket and bedroll. He recognized that he'd probably had the same look as a boy, but it went deeper than bone. And while he wasn't ready to say it and Tony wasn't nearly ready to hear it, he was pretty damn sure that the word for what he was feeling right now was love.

Jeannie would just die if she knew their son had confronted him like that, Rafe realized. She'd called him twice since she'd come to see him in San Antonio, once to tell him to bring his saddle if he still had it and the other time to ask if he'd be there in time for Sunday dinner.

He smiled as he deposited the last of his gear in the stall and left the barn, remembering how excited she'd sounded on the phone. She dearly wanted him and Tony to get along. Hell, *he* wanted that too. But one thing he'd learned in the practice of the law was that an easy remedy was a rare commodity. And the harder a case was to prepare, the greater his satisfaction in winning it.

Time and patience, those were the keys. Just as he had to build his legal cases with painstaking care, so he would have to build a loving relationship with his son. He closed the trunk lid with a decided slam, knowing he was in for the long haul.

As for Jeannie—

"The Studebaker!"

Rafe spun around just as Jeannie came down the porch steps and started across the ranch yard. From a distance she looked about eighteen again. But as she got closer, he realized she looked better than that. She looked womanly and welcoming and good enough to eat.

She wore a gauzy sundress in a hot peach shade that set her fluid figure off to perfection. The bodice crisscrossed over her breasts and tied behind her neck, leaving her back and shoulders bare. A kerchief hem flirted fashionably with her knees, while strappy sandals paid homage to her slender feet.

An anarchy of waves, her hair rioted freely about her oval face. Subtly applied makeup deepened the smoky mystery of her eyes at the same time it highlighted the sensual promise of her mouth. A gold bracelet snaked around one wrist, and huge hoop earrings swayed to the enticing rhythm of her stride.

"I can't believe you still have it," she marveled as she marched straight to the Studebaker and rubbed her palm along its smoothly painted rear fender.

Rafe studied her stroking hand and found himself envying his own damned car. "I keep it in storage and only break it out for special occasions."

Jeannie looked up, her eyes the color of the creek at dusk. Much as a lover's fingers would do, as his fingers wanted to do, the warm breeze tossed the loose waves of her hair. Her mouth, moist and peachy and tempting as all get-out, curved in a smile that sent his body temperature soaring a good twenty degrees.

"I'm glad you consider this a special occasion." Her voice was soft, as soft as the lips he would have kissed right then and there if a pickup truck hadn't rumbled into the ranch yard and a cowhand hadn't climbed out and begun loading bags of cattle feed into the back of it not fifty feet from where they stood.

He settled for brushing a finger over the gold hoop in her ear. Then he issued her both a crooked smile and a casual invitation. "Wanna take a ride?"

"I'd love to!"

He cut around to the passenger side and opened her door. "Your chariot awaits."

"Where're we going?" she asked before she got in.

"To the fourplex."

She dropped her gaze to the dusty ground between her sandals and his boots, but not before he saw the disappointment that had clouded her eyes. "I told you when I called that you were welcome to stay at the house."

He slid his index finger under her chin and eased it upward until he could see her face. "Aren't you forgetting something?"

"What?"

"Tony."

Jeannie made a moue of regret, whether in response to his lowering his hand or the boom he couldn't even begin to guess. "You'd have your own room, of course."

It was ironic, Rafe thought, that after all this time and all he'd experienced he should have to be the one to say, "How long do you think I'd stay there, knowing you were just across the hall?"

She leaned into him, a pale lily seeking the sun. "With branding starting tomorrow, Tony will be asleep by nine."

And with the delicate buds of her breasts quivering against his chest, he was hard-pressed not to bring them to full flower. "How would he react to finding me—a man he's only met one other time—in his mother's bed tomorrow morning?"

"I'll tell him who you are tonight." Her warm breath swirled with his, rushing his senses, eroding his resistance.

But remembering that showdown with Tony in the barn a few moments ago, he stuck to his guns. "I don't think he's quite ready to hear it."

Having exhausted her store of womanly wiles, not to mention the willpower of the man she'd been practicing them on, Jeannie gave up and got in the car. "I guess you're right."

"I *know* I'm right." Without further elaboration, Rafe closed the passenger door and cut around to the driver's side.

She waited until he was situated behind the wheel before she asked, "I take it you've already seen Tony?"

"Just briefly."

"Well, what do you think of your progeny?"

He couldn't tell her what he really thought without beating a dead horse, so he opted for the easy way out. "I think he's hell on wheels."

She laughed, exactly the reaction he'd hoped to elicit. "Like father, like son."

"Lord help us," he muttered under his breath as he pulled away from the barn.

Her smile faltered when he braked to a stop in front of the fourplex and cut the motor. "Do you need some help unloading the car?"

"No, thanks." He pocketed the keys and thumbed toward the back, where his suitbag hung. "That's all I have to carry in."

"What day do you have to go to court?"

"Wednesday."

"You'll be back that night, though?"

Rafe saw the glint of anxiety in her gray eyes and told himself that it was to be expected, given the way he'd just up and disappeared on her eleven years ago. It occurred to him then that Tony wasn't the only one whose trust he had to win. There were a few chinks that he needed to repair in his foundation with Jeannie too.

"I'll be back that night with bells on," he promised solemnly.

She reached for her doorhandle. "Just gun the motor, and I'll come running."

But this time, by God, they were going to do it right. This time they weren't waiting till dark for fear of being seen together. And this time he was coming to her.

"If you'll wait for me," he said as he opened his door, "I'll hang my suitbag in the closet and then walk you back to the house."

Her smile came back, urging him to hurry.

The two-and-a-half-room apartment, which had been sitting empty since its previous occupant moved on to the greener pastures of marriage, was a far cry from his loft, where he had every convenience at his fingertips. Here the kitchen consisted of little more than a teakettle and a hot plate, the bathroom was barely big enough to turn around in, and the bedroom was a virtual monk's cell. But it was clean. And when he looked out the window and saw the woman waiting for him on the front stoop, he suddenly realized it was home.

"And what's this?"

"Tony on his first day of kindergarten and me on my first day of college."

Rafe smiled at the photograph and rubbed

his fingertips over it. "You look more like his older sister or his baby-sitter than you do his mother."

Jeannie laughed. "By the time I got him ready to go, all I had time to do was put my hair in a ponytail, grab my books, and jump in the car."

They were sitting on the living room sofa, waiting for Martha to call them to dinner and browsing through the picture album that chronicled everything from Tony's first footprints—"So tiny!" Rafe had marveled—to his first birthday cake—"Such a mess," Jeannie had moaned—to his first day of school.

"It must have been rough," he said now, "taking care of a growing boy and carrying a full load of classes all at the same time."

"It was," she agreed, remembering those frantic days more fondly from a distance. "But I was determined to graduate from college in the same century I'd graduated from high school."

He grinned his congratulations and turned the page.

She glanced at the picture and spotted trouble.

Looking at the album had been an emotional experience for both of them. They'd exchanged proud "ah's" over their son's baptismal photographs and shared words of solace at the last snapshot of his first dog before it was hit by a car out on the highway. But whenever they came to a picture of Big Tom with Tony, as they had now, they lapsed into silence.

Rafe flipped through the remaining pages without further comment, then closed the album. Jeannie replaced it on the built-in bookshelf, almost wishing she'd never gotten it out, and resumed her seat on the sofa.

"I'm sorry." He slipped an arm around her shoulders and drew her closer. "It just fries me to think that while I was trying to keep some client out of the pokey, a man who despised me was teaching my son to ride a pony."

"I understand." Curling her legs beneath her, she nestled consolingly against his hard frame. "But you saw with your own eyes what good buddies they were and how much fun they had together."

Rafe checked the angry response that came to his lips. There was nothing to be gained by lashing out at Jeannie. She'd loved her father, warts and all. And as much as he hated to admit it, a part of him would always be grateful to Big Tom for the advantages and affection he'd given Tony.

A *very small* part of him, he qualified silently before saying in a wry voice, "Yeah, they were a pair to draw to, all right."

"Butch Cassidy and the Sundance Kid," she quipped.

"Cisco and Pancho," he shot back.

She laughed, a rich, smoky sound, and he felt the tension ease. He tightened his arm, telling her wordlessly that he wanted her closer, and she rested her head against his chest.

The slowly rotating blades of the ceiling fan chased away yet another of yesterday's clouds as they sat there, while the late-afternoon sunlight filtering in through the white wooden shutters promised a brighter tomorrow.

Rafe's thumb began making lazy circles on Jeannie's bare arm. Her forefinger returned the favor, drawing loops and fairy rings along the muscular length of his thigh.

"I want you," he whispered roughly, stirring her hair with his harsh statement.

She lifted her head and smiled up at him, saying softly, "You've got me."

His lips came down on hers. Moist heat flared along the curves of her mouth as he traced them with his tongue. She made a small yearning sound and met his tongue with her own, twining, and her sweet, sweet taste was a banquet after a long fast.

One of his hands moved to cover her breast and massage it gently through the gauzy bodice. The other dived into her daffodil hair to comb and toy with the rebellious locks. Her fingers gave his silver earring a twirl before going on to explore the taut column of his neck and the supple muscles of his shoulders and back. Even when the kiss ended and they came up for air, their long-denied bodies continued to clamor for the ultimate closeness.

"Ohhh, Cisco," she breathed as the friction from the back of his knuckle brought her nipple to a tight peak.

"Ohhh, Pancho," he rasped when she reached down and laid her open hand over his bulging fly.

Their silliness gave way to seriousness then as they gazed deeply into each other's eyes, drinking in the sights they'd sorely missed these last eleven years, drenching themselves in feelings too powerful to be voiced.

Jeannie pulled her hand away and looped her arms around Rafe's neck, tangling her fingers in the thick and silky waves of hair at his nape. His hands shifted to her back, his palms caressing her warm, bare skin as he drew her nearer. Moving of one accord then, they tipped their heads until their lips met again.

Their loving reunion came to an end when, simultaneously, they realized that their thundering heartbeats weren't all that they heard. Bootsteps, slowing from a loping run down the hall to a screeching halt in the living room doorway, broke them apart. And belligerent blue eyes fairly shouted disapproval when the startled couple looked to find their son standing there staring at them.

"Dinner's ready," Tony announced abruptly.

Ten

Dinner was a disaster.

Jeannie couldn't fault the food. To the contrary, Martha's pot roast was fork-tender and her mashed potatoes butter-melting fluffy. Her hot rolls were the yeastiest yet, perfect for dipping in the savory beef gravy, and her coconut cake could have won any bake-off hands down.

No, it wasn't the meal that made Jeannie's tongue cleave to the roof of her mouth with every bite and her throat rebel against swallowing. It was the demeanor of her male companions. And it was the table conversation—or, more accurately—the *lack* of conversation among them.

Rafe had tried to get the ball rolling. He'd asked Tony all kinds of questions about school, wanting to know which subjects he liked best, who his favorite teachers were, and what sports he played. But Tony, who could talk the leg off a chair if the spirit moved him, had turned into a monosyllabic wonder. And Rusty, not really loquacious to begin with, had literally eaten in silence.

Jeannie had planned on this week being a turning point. The end to bitterness as father and son finally made each other's acquaintance and began to form a bond. A rebirth of the sweet life as Rafe and she took advantage of this second chance they'd been miraculously afforded.

What she hadn't planned on was Tony's animosity.

Granted he was still grieving for his grandfather. And he must have been terribly surprised to find his mother in such a compromising position with a man he hardly knew. But his rudeness went beyond sorrow or shock, almost bordering on resentment.

So now, with the cake plates sitting empty and Martha pouring coffee, Jeannie's great expectations had shrunk to the size of the coconut crumbs littering the linen tablecloth.

As she lifted her cup to her lips, her eyes inadvertently met Rafe's. He was sitting across the table from her, the very enactment of her fantasies in a casual white shirt that complemented both his coloring and his broad shoulders. Despite the sartorial elegance, his tanned face was a picture of patience and pain. She loved him so much she ached with it. And it broke her heart to think that their son didn't even like him.

Dropping her gaze, she set her cup back down on its matching saucer. The yellow primrose pattern on the china suddenly reminded her of something she'd meant to bring up earlier.

Jeannie glanced around her with a hopeful smile. "Does anyone happen to know where that yellow rose on my mother's grave came from?"

Rafe shook his head. Tony shrugged and went back to balancing his fork between two fingers, obviously killing time until he could be excused from the table. Rusty spilled his coffee and immediately cursed the arthritis that made him so clumsy. Then he apologized for cursing.

Martha rushed to the ranch manager's aid. After checking to be certain he hadn't burned his hand, she pulled a paper towel from her apron pocket and used it to soak up the brown lake in his saucer.

"There was another rose?" she asked as she finished mopping up and refilled Rusty's cup.

"Yesterday morning." When she'd first seen it from her bedroom window, Jeannie hadn't given it a second thought. Every Saturday for almost eighteen years she had awakened to find a single yellow rose lying at the base of

Laurrinda Crane's tombstone. As the day wore on, though, she'd begun to wonder how it had gotten there. Big Tom was dead. So, unless his reach extended beyond the grave—

"Call the florist in Bolero," Rafe suggested.

"I did, yesterday afternoon," Jeannie told him. "I figured Big Tom might have had a standing order, and I thought I'd cancel any future orders and settle the bill."

"What did he say?"

"He said Big Tom had never ordered any roses from him."

Martha looked thoroughly baffled now. "That's odd."

Jeannie nodded. "Isn't it, though?"

"What makes you think it was Grandpa who was putting the roses on Grandma's grave?" Tony seemed intrigued enough by this mini-mystery to string more than two syllables together.

Good question, Jeannie thought. And one she really didn't have a real good answer for. She lifted her bare shoulders in a helpless shrug and said, "Well, he was her husband."

"Yeah, but maybe somebody else—"

"If you all will excuse me," Rusty interrupted, scraping his chair back and standing up, "I've got a couple of hundred bawling calves that need a baby-sitter, so I'd better call it a night."

"Can I sleep out with you?" Tony wasn't as close to the foreman as he had been to his grandfather, but he was always ready for an adventure.

"Not tonight."

"Then when?"

Rusty smiled—a little sadly, Jeannie thought—as he reached over to ruffle Tony's hair. "Maybe Tuesday or Wednesday, if you work real hard and if it's all right with your mama."

"Wednesday night would be best," Jeannie said, remembering that Rafe would be spending the day in court and probably wouldn't be back till late. Remembering, too, that he'd promised he'd be back with bells on . . . bells she intended to ring to her heart's content.

"Fine," Rusty agreed before bidding them all good night and heading for the front door.

"Well," Tony said around a huge fake yawn that failed to hide his excitement over the prospect of camping out with the cowhands, "I guess I'll go to bed now too."

Martha reminded everyone that breakfast was at sunup, and not a minute sooner, before she gathered the empty plates and cups and carried them out to the kitchen.

"That little stinker," Jeannie said through gritted teeth as the sound of Tony's bedroom door banging shut echoed back down to the living room. "He didn't even kiss me good night."

Rafe reached across the table and took her hand. The light from the crystal chandelier shone down on the raw black silk of his hair. "I'm afraid our son is angry at both of us."

"Because of what he saw in the living room?" she asked, staring at the buttons on his shirt.

"That's part of the problem." His voice was as gravelly and emotion-packed as hers.

"What other reason could he possibly have?"

"I'm sitting in Big Tom's place, and you put me here."

She studied the hand that held hers—engulfed it, actually. Neatly trimmed nails tipped the long, lean fingers. Blue veins corded the burnt-sienna skin. Dark hairs swooped down from that strong wrist. "What are we going to do about it?"

The latter should take care of itself, since we'll be eating most of our meals in camp."

Jeannie was afraid she already knew the answer to her next question, but she asked it anyway. "And the former?"

Rafe's thumb traveled the peaks and valleys of her knuckles, taking her stomach along for the ride. "I think we'd better cool it for a while."

"How long is 'a while'?"

"A couple of days."

She sighed in disappointment. "And nights."

" 'Fraid so."

"How do you feel about children going to visit their relatives over spring break?"

He laughed, a throaty sound that told her he shared her frustration. "I think travel broadens their horizons."

"I'll pack his clothes." Jeannie was only joking, but the idea had merit.

Rafe dipped his finger into the hollow of the fist she'd made of her hand, causing her to squirm in her seat. "And I'll drive him to your aunt's in Houston."

Their conversation had dropped to an intimate pitch as the sexual tension had mounted between them.

Her head came up and she forgot all about their refractory son as her world narrowed down to the man who had fathered him. She could see the longing in his deep-blue eyes, a longing that rippled through her entire body to the farthest extremity of her soul, and she wanted nothing more at that moment than to fulfill their mutual desires.

But he released her hand and with a rueful smile said, "Well, I guess if I'm going to get up with the cows, I'd better go to bed with the chickens."

As he rose from the table and replaced his chair, she stared at him in disbelief. She had to swallow hard before saying hoarsely, "You're leaving?"

"Walk me to the door?" he asked, cutting around the table to stand politely behind her.

With him all but pulling her chair out from

under her, what other recourse did she have? "Of course."

Rather than stopping at the door, she walked him out to the porch. The sun was but a memory, having made its exit a little over an hour ago. A gold doubloon of a moon outshone the silver shower of stars. That perpetual Texas breeze blew a warm promise for the morrow.

It was a night for fond farewells, for lovers to be clinging regretfully and whispering romantically, seasoning the fecund air with spring fancies and sweet nothings.

Jeannie just knew that Rafe was going to kiss her before he left her, and she was really primed for it. She tipped her head back, the better to accommodate his firm mouth upon her pliant one, and moistened her lips with the tip of her tongue in feverish anticipation.

It came as a complete shock when, instead, he cuffed her lightly under the chin and said a soft "good night" before turning and bounding down the porch steps.

Crestfallen, she watched him disappear into the night, realizing suddenly that starting over again could be the pits.

The bedroom light came on, shining invitingly through an aluminum screen and a swirl of antique lace.

A woman wearing a slither of a white silk

nightgown, her golden hair spilling in siren's waves to her bare shoulders, stepped to the window. She stood perfectly still for a moment, her gray eyes trying to pierce the darkness below, her head tilted as if listening for something . . . a signal perhaps.

A bullfrog concert came faintly from the creek bank. Whippoorwills piped their prairie lullabye for lowing calves and lonesome cowboys. Cicadas churred a song of their own.

But otherwise all was silent.

A man, drawn like some hapless summer insect by that rectangular patch of light, stood stock-still in the shadows cast by the spreading tree branches beneath the window. A rock, worn smooth by wind and rain, fire and frost, burned a hole in the palm of his hand. All he had to do was throw it and the woman would come running.

But he couldn't bring himself to throw it. Couldn't force himself to move away either. He could only remain as he was, completely bewitched by the beauty who owned his soul.

Her hair—the sun of his heart, the source of his heat—gleamed from repeated brushings and rippled like golden threads to her shoulders. The bodice of her nightgown, held up by straps as fine as mandolin strings, cupped her full breasts. Her nipples, the enticing hollow of her navel, her hips, the exciting vee

where her legs came together . . . all knew
the kiss of white silk.

The man grew hard, his palm slippery, and
that rock grew heavier with every passing
minute.

The woman held her listening pose for a
little while longer before she turned away from
the window and turned off the light.

The man watched the window go dark before dropping that damn rock and moving
deeper into the shadows.

•

Eleven

"Can I try?" Blue eyes dancing with excitement, Tony reached for the handle of the branding iron, which glowed a dull red in the campfire.

"*No!*" Rafe reacted instinctively, grabbing the boy's wrist and yanking his hand back from the hot rod.

Jeannie, her heart galloping like a wild horse in her chest at the thought of how close he'd come to burning himself, said gently, "You forgot to put your gloves on, honey."

Twin flags of embarrassment stained Tony's cheeks as he reached into the back pocket of his jeans for the work gloves he'd taken off at lunchtime.

Orchestrated chaos prevailed in the camp. Dust clogged the nostrils of humans and horses alike. Calves lowed plaintively for their

mothers, cows for their offspring. The afternoon sun burned a brand of its own into the
backs of unprotected necks and hands.

"Now you're ready," Rafe said, motioning a
regloved Tony over to the campfire so that he
could teach him the trick of making a clean
brand on the calf being wrestled to the ground.

But the boy was either still smarting over
his earlier gaffe or he was digging his heels in
deeper as the day grew longer. Maybe a little of
both. Whatever, he scuffed the toe of his boot
in the dirt and shook his head. "I want Rusty
to show me."

"Rusty's busy vaccinating the calves." Jeannie realized that it wasn't her place to interfere,
but he was up to his old tricks again, and she
was almost at the end of her rope in the patience department. "So why don't you let
Rafe—"

"I'll wait for Rusty," Tony said sullenly, then
turned and walked away.

He knows, Jeannie thought, her irritation
collapsing under a mother lode of love and guilt
as she watched him take up his post at the
kneeling ranch manager's shoulder. Somehow
he knows and he's just trying to sort things out.

Rafe, surprisingly enough, seemed to be taking Tony's reticence in stride. He grabbed the
branding iron and, wielding it with all the ex-
pertise of old, pressed its glowing red end firmly
onto the exposed flank of the Hereford calf.

"Let 'im up," he ordered, stepping back from

the bawling calf who now wore the Circle C brand and nodding to the man holding the frightened animal down.

The cowhand let go, and the calf scrambled to all fours. No sooner had the first Hereford hightailed it out of there than a second was dragged kicking and baw-w-w-wing to the ground to be vaccinated and branded.

Calf after calf, it went like clockwork.

Jeannie didn't notice the way Rafe's lean muscles rippled beneath his blue chambray work shirt when he knelt to sear the hot brand into the calf's hide. Nor did she pay any attention to how red and sunburned Tony's nose was getting as he helped Rusty with the vaccination. All she saw were a man and a boy keeping a painfully polite distance within the tightly knit circle.

Suddenly she wanted to scream at both of them. At Tony for his stubborn rejection and at Rafe for his stoic acceptance. Father and son were tearing her apart, much as father and lover had all those years ago. And she either had to get away or go crazy.

"You take over the ear tagging," she told one of the cowhands. "I'm going to look for strays." Then she gathered the reins to her horse, swung into the saddle, and rode out of camp.

Jeannie had made her escape with a perfectly legitimate excuse. Mavericks often concealed themselves from the roundup crew, taking cover in the scrub oaks and shrubby mesquite trees that crowned the rocky hills or in the tall cottonwoods and knobby cypresses that lined the creek bank. Accordingly she made a last sweeping search of the areas where they were most likely to hide.

After an hour of beating the bushes, she hadn't come up with any strays but she had calmed down considerably. Her mare, a gleaming chestnut she'd trained herself, whickered softly and tugged at the bit as they approached the creek.

"Thirsty, girl?" Jeannie asked as she dismounted and led her horse toward the silvery rush of water that was fed by the Guadalupe River.

Listening to the mare suck in the liquid in noisy slurps, she realized her own mouth felt dry. She removed her hat, a straw Stetson, and laid it on the ground. Then she shook her hair free after hours of being tucked up under the crown, rolled back the sleeves of the oversize white cotton shirt she'd knotted at her waist, and stretched flat on her stomach on the grassy bank to get a drink.

The water, which she scooped up with one hand while keeping hold of the reins with the other, was spring-thaw cold and so clear she could see the glistening rocks on the creek bottom.

Jeannie had just taken her last drink when she felt a pull on the reins. She tightened her grip and looked up to find that the chestnut had lifted its head in sudden alertness. As she pushed to her feet, she heard the drumming of a horse's hooves fast approaching.

Rafe slowed the restive black gelding he'd chosen from the working remuda that morning to a long-striding walk when he saw her standing there. He sat tall and straight in the saddle, his strong hands controlling the reins and his lean thighs straddling the broad back of his mount.

A crow cried in alarm as he guided the gelding into the clearing. Squirrels scampered for cover. Even the leaves on the cottonwoods and cypresses trembled in his wake.

From the red bandanna holding his ebony hair back to the spiky rowels on his spurs, he looked like a *comanchero* riding out of the Old West and into the New. His coppery skin, dark beard stubble, and bold smile all served to reinforce the image. As did the silver-bladed knife sheathed at his belt.

His smile widened as his glance skimmed from the bits of green still clinging to the front of her shirt to the grass-stained knees of her jeans. "Been lying down on the job, I see."

Jeannie dropped the reins and raised her palms in a gesture of surrender. "Caught red-handed."

"*Wet*-handed is more like it." Laughing now, Rafe lithely dismounted and let his horse dip its nose into the clear-running creek.

She could feel the swift pace of the blood in

her veins as he leisurely approached her. Wiping the palm of her damp hand on the seat of her pants, she shrugged and said, "I got so thirsty looking for strays, I decided to stop and get a drink."

"Did you find any?" A lazily seductive gleam entered his blue eyes as he plucked a blade of grass from her cotton-covered breast.

"Not a one." Her voice slipped a notch when he lifted yet another piece of green, this time from the tail of the knot over her bare stomach.

"Too bad." His thumb moved up to the deep vee of her neckline to whisk away a blade stuck to her first button.

"Mmm-hmm . . ." Pleasure burgeoned in her lower body when his hand slid to the second button.

Slowly but thoroughly, as if he had an eternity to complete the project, he picked her shirt clean. The light touch of his dark fingers was both physically and visually stimulating. By the time he finished, her nipples had tightened into hard points against the soft cloth, and her gray eyes held the turbulence of desire long denied.

They hadn't been alone all day. At the breakfast table they'd been surrounded by a half dozen hungry cowboys. In the barn Rusty had been issuing orders left and right. During branding, Tony had been as daunting as a bad conscience.

Now it was just Rafe and Jeannie. One man and one woman.

"Come here," he said gruffly.

She gladly obeyed his command.

This was no gentle embrace they shared. He caught her cornsilk hair in one hand, clamped the other over the bare skin between her shirt and jeans, and jerked her against him. She dug her nails into the ropy muscles of his back, and arched into him.

Nor was this the tender kiss that every giddy teenage girl dreamed of and every awkward adolescent boy wanted to get just right. This was an open-mouthed, tongue-thrusting, teeth-grazing act of adult passion and raw need.

Jeannie reveled in the savage male essence of Rafe. He smelled of saddle leather and sweat. Tasted of salt. His heart slammed like a blacksmith's hammer against her breasts. And he was so rigid with want, she couldn't tell where the knife at his belt ended and his body began.

Together, with mouths clinging, they dropped to their knees on the creek bank.

He released her hair and gripped her shoulders between his hands, angling her backward. She relaxed the curled tension of her fingers as she landed on a bed of grass. When he stretched out on top of her, she opened her thighs. He burrowed, hot and hard, against her warm, welcoming softness.

Only when their lungs threatened to burst for the lack of air did their mouths break apart.

He raised his head. She tipped hers back.

Rapidly breathing they stared into each other's eyes—his glittering like sapphires in his swarthy face; hers as dark as burnt silver beneath her half-closed lashes.

"I listened for you last night," she whispered.

"I saw you at the window," he admitted throatily.

"Wh—" She stopped herself from asking why he hadn't signaled her, knowing instinctively that he wouldn't have wanted to risk waking Tony in the room next to hers. "What were you thinking?"

Rafe smiled his hombre's smile and sat back on his heels. "That I wanted to see you up close."

Jeannie's stomach muscles constricted in sensual suspense as he made short work of the knot at her waist and the buttons on her shirt.

He laid the soft cotton open and laughed.

She frowned up at him. "What's so funny?"

He released her wispy bra's front clasp with a flick of his fingers. "Only you would wear lace for branding."

She raised her knees, hugging his lean hips between them. "Ah, but look at the maverick I caught."

The creek babbled anxiously, echoing her heartbeat, as he peeled back the sheer shells and exposed, for his eyes only, the alabaster perfection of her breasts.

For a burning moment he did nothing more than look his fill. Yielding to her silent yearning then, he lowered his dark head and drew her dusky nipple into his mouth.

She gave a shuddering cry and gripped his head with both hands, holding it against her. Her back arched off the ground as he circled her and suckled her, using his tongue and teeth and lips to take her higher than she'd ever gone before.

A thousand forgotten feelings swept over Jeannie as Rafe kissed his way across her chest, to claim her other breast. She shuddered with rising excitement when his tongue fluttered back and forth and all around the rosy tip. His fingers, as deft and daring as ever, continued to fondle the swollen crest he'd just aroused.

"Sweet," he breathed hotly against her highly sensitized skin. And then, as though English couldn't possibly express his emotions, he murmured, *"Dulce . . . dulce."*

Oh, and it was sweet, so sweet, to be held and kissed and caressed by the only man who knew her inside out. To hold and kiss and caress him in return . . .

She slipped off his bandanna and felt his hair fall over her hands. Black silk. She bent her head and touched her lips to his earring. Warm silver. She reached between them and unbuttoned his shirt. Furred strength.

He moaned deeply, more vibration than sound, when her fingers made contact with his turgid nipples. Then his head came back up and he covered her mouth with his, the velvet rapier of his tongue engaging hers in an erotic duel in which there were no losers, only winners.

Their bodies, joined from lips to hips but still separated by the denim barriers of their jeans, found that wonderful mating rhythm that made the world go around. But after eleven years apart, it wasn't enough. Not nearly enough. They needed to know each other in the fullest sense. They needed to know each other in the flesh.

Rafe broke off the kiss and raised his head, staring down at her with naked desire. "I want you, Jeannie."

"I want you too," she whispered, looking up at him with a love undimmed by time, untarnished by treachery.

Was it the sighing breeze or the twin rasps of their zippers that breached the stillness of the clearing? Was it the leaf-filtered sunlight or the smoldering gaze of the man that gave the skin she bared such a rosy glow? Was it the spring heat or the long-awaited sight of the woman that caused the breath in his lungs to catch fire?

"You're even more beautiful than I remembered," Rafe said, his voice rich and low as he cupped the round globe of her breast, smoothed the silken plane of her stomach, sought the swollen folds beneath the golden curls nesting between her legs.

"So are you." Jeannie returned the compliment, marveling at the strength and the power of him as she caressed his muscular back, praised his runner's buttocks, found the bold proof of his desire for her with a gentle fist and a glad refrain, "So are you."

Time spiraled in reverse when he rolled her to her back and braced himself above her. The wasted years simply slipped away as she arched her hips to meet the thrust of his, then caught a breath of mingled pleasure and pain.

Rafe was instantly aware of why she tensed. He stopped, ecstatic disbelief flaring in his blue-ribbon eyes as he searched her flushed face. "I thought you and Webb—"

"You thought wrong." Jeannie's lips curved in a loving smile as her body conformed to his with a silent entreaty. "Don't hold anything back. I want all of you."

All of him was what she got. He was hard and hot and supremely male. And all of herself was what she gave. She was soft and dewy and splendidly female.

They watched each other as he entered her. Kissed each other when they were finally one. Whispered to each other in a mixture of Spanish and English as they moved in unison.

"Jeannie . . . *querida* . . ."

"Rafe . . . my love . . ."

He'd been the first for her, and she for him. Together again, they found the lasting fulfillment they'd thought was forever lost to them.

"Did I hurt you?"

"No. Why?"

Rafe bent his head and kissed away the tears that sparkled on her cheeks. "You're crying."

Jeannie reached up and touched his lower lip with her forefinger. "Tears of joy."

He frowned and nipped her finger with his strong white teeth. "Maybe twice was too much."

She smiled and snuggled contentedly to his naked length. "No way, Jose."

They'd loved and laughed and, after rinsing off in the cold, clear creek, they'd loved again. Now they lay with arms and legs entwined, relishing the delicious feeling of skin on skin and the utter rightness of being together again.

But trite as it sounded, all good things had to come to an end. And though neither of them wanted to admit it—not just yet anyway—both of them knew their stolen hour was ticking away without regard for their hearts' wishes.

Rafe finally made the first move, the one Jeannie couldn't bring herself to make. He brushed the hair back from her damp face and pressed his lips to her brow in a lingering kiss. Then he reluctantly disengaged himself from her possessive embrace and helped her to her feet.

"If we don't get a move on," he said as he started putting on his clothes and his boots, "Rusty's liable to send a search party after us."

"Or worse yet," she said, reaching for her bra and panties and inadvertantly hitting a raw nerve in the process, "Tony might come looking for us."

"Yeah." He zipped up his jeans with a terse movement but made no effort to rebutton his shirt. "God forbid our son should find us together again."

They stood only a few feet apart, but she could feel the spiritual distance growing between them, yawning wide as a gulf. She racked her brain as she finished dressing, wishing she'd kept her mouth shut and desperate to find a way to keep him from slipping farther away from her.

Rafe picked up the bandanna she'd slipped off him in the heat of passion and twisted it before retying it around his forehead. "I wanted to strangle you when I first found out about Tony. . . ."

Jeannie shivered as he let the thought trail off but left the threat hanging between them. She knew he would never harm her physically, that he was just as heartsore as she was at the way Tony was behaving, yet she couldn't stop one hand from fluttering up to her throat.

"And now?" she asked tautly.

He gave her a rebellious look that resembled Tony at his worst. "And now I just want to get the hell out of here before he shows up and starts glaring daggers at me."

She didn't even realize how much she was counting on his saying that he wanted Tony to love him until he smarted off like that. Caution told her the moment had come to back off, but she couldn't do it, not with something this important at stake. Not when she felt his need as deeply as she felt her own.

Dropping her hand, she pleaded both her case and Tony's. "Give him time, Rafe."

"I've given him plenty of time, Jeannie."

"Two days?"

A bitter smile shunted across the alluring mouth that only moments before had brought her the most exquisite pleasure she'd ever experienced. "Long enough for him to decide he hates me."

"He doesn't hate you."

"Couldn't prove it by me."

"He's just a confused little boy—"

"With a big chip on his shoulder."

"He'll come around."

"When hell freezes over."

Jeannie shivered, despite the rising temperature, and crossed her arms over her breasts. Rafe just stood there, every muscle in his body taut with belligerence, and she wondered what other surprises he had in store for her.

He ended the suspense by saying, "I've decided I'm not going to run for the state senate."

Stunned, she could only stare at him for a moment before crying, "What?"

He returned her incredulous look with a level one of his own. "You heard me."

"Yes." She nodded, then shook her head, still trying to assimilate his news. "But—"

"But nothing." The note of finality in his voice said he'd already made up his mind and there was absolutely no use in her arguing with him about it. "When I get through in court on Wednesday, I'm going to call a press conference and close down my campaign headquarters."

"Score one for Big Tom." Jeannie hadn't planned on saying that; the words had just popped out of her mouth. But under the circumstances they certainly seemed appropriate.

Rafe scowled. "What's that supposed to mean?"

"After reading that personality piece on you in the newspaper—the one where they quoted you as saying you jogged to help you relax—"

"I know the one you're talking about."

"Big Tom said you ought to forget trying to win an election and concentrate on winning a marathon."

A muscle jumped in Rafe's jaw as the analogy sank in. "That rotten son of a—"

"He said your long legs would serve you better than your legal education any day."

"I don't have to stand here and listen to that—"

"Don't you dare turn your back on me, Rafe Martinez!" Jeannie shouted when he rounded on his heel and started walking across the clearing. "Especially after dropping a bomb like you just dropped!"

Halfway to the low-hanging tree limb where he'd tethered their horses a little earlier, he stopped and squared around. The cool blue of his eyes and the hard expression on his face warned her she was pushing her luck, but she paid those signs no heed.

"You owe me, dammit." She ran a frantic hand through her tangled hair. "You're the man I love. The father of my son. And after the wonderful hour we just spent in each other's arms, the least you owe me is a credible explanation for why you're giving up your lifelong dream."

"I don't owe you anything but a lump-sum payment for the past ten years and a monthly child-support check for the next eight." His nostrils flared on a harsh breath. "Naturally I'll pick up the bill for Tony's college tuition, too, should he decide he wants to go."

Jeannie recoiled as though Rafe had struck her. And in a very real way he had. He'd delivered a verbal backhand to her heart.

Tears of hurt and anger stung her eyes, mixing together, as she watched him turn and walk away. Suddenly all the loss and the sadness—the death of her mother, her father's deception, the desertions by the boy who'd been her first love and the man who was her last—became twisted into a Byzantine rope of pain that choked her and chafed her and rent her in two. And something inside of her snapped.

"Go on—run!" she said tauntingly as he swung into the saddle. "Run from the immigration authorities!" She felt the tears on her cheeks and impatiently brushed them away.

"Run from the voters who just might forgive you a youthful indiscretion if you're honest with them about what happened!"

"And then what?" he said jeeringly over his shoulder.

Jeannie's eyes went cloudy with confusion. "What do you mean 'and then what'?"

Rafe half-turned in the saddle, a trenchant smile twisting his lips. "I mean after I make a clean breast of it, what am I supposed to do? Stand idly by and watch the media vultures swoop down on you and Tony?"

"I can take it," she protested, relief flooding through her at the realization that they'd finally gotten to the root of his problem. "And the two of us, working together, can protect Tony from the worst of it."

"I'm tired of protecting other people." His voice was flat, without emotion, as though he were speaking from a void somewhere deep inside him.

"But Tony is your son!"

"Biologically yes."

"Wh-what are you saying?" she all but croaked.

"I'm saying that in every other way, Tony is Big Tom's son—a Crane, not a Martinez."

Shock rendered her speechless. Her knees threatened to buckle. And her heart—oh, her poor heart!—leapt with quick, shallow beats, like a stone skipping over the surface of a pond.

"Now, if you'll excuse me, ma'am," he said mockingly as he turned in the saddle and angled his horse toward the edge of the clearing, "I've got work to do."

Driven by the knowledge that she'd already lost him, she charged across the bed of grass that still bore the imprint of their entwined bodies and took a wild swing at his stirrup. "Go on, you—"

The gelding, startled by her sudden move, shied and danced sideways, checking her outburst and causing her to jump backward, out of harm's way.

Rafe reined his frightened mount around with a firm hand and stared down at her with eyes that glinted like blue steel in the sun-dappled shade of the clearing. "Finish your sentence, Jeannie," he challenged in a raw fury. "'Go on, you' . . ."

She knew that later she would deeply regret the parting words she flung up in his face. But now, right now, she was too filled with pain to care what she said.

"Go on, greaser." She pointed a rigid finger at the path of least resistance. "Run from the responsibility of telling your son who and what you are."

His nostrils flaring with pride, he reined the gelding around and did exactly that.

The bedroom light didn't come on. Nor did the woman come to the window. And the man standing in the shadows below had no one but himself to blame.

Twelve

"Easy does it, Lady," Jeannie whispered as she finished tying the pregnant mare's tail out of the way with a gauze strip. "It'll be over before you know it."

Lying on her side on a fresh layer of wheat and rye straw, Lady was ready to foal. Alternately panting and pushing, she'd been in heavy labor for a good half hour.

"Believe it or not," Jeannie said, sinking to her knees on the stall floor and stroking the mare's velvety-soft muzzle, "you won't even remember the pain."

The horse whinnied shrilly, as if to say she would always remember the pain, and her human birthing partner had to laugh.

When she'd ridden in from branding camp last night, Jeannie had noticed that the mare was sweating over her shoulders and flanks and kicking at her sides. Still upset after that fight with Rafe, and knowing that she wasn't going to be able to sleep anyway, she'd decided to bed down in the barn.

She was really glad now that she'd done it. Not only was foaling her favorite event, a sign from God that life went on even in the midst of tragedy, but helping Lady in her time of travail had helped her to forget—for a little while at least—the guilt she felt over that terrible name she'd called Rafe.

He'd provoked her into doing it. Dared her, in fact. That was no excuse, though. She shouldn't have even thought it, much less said it. But to her everlasting shame, she'd done both. Now the only choice she had was to apologize. Tell him how sorry she was. And pray he forgave her.

Lady began to push in earnest, snapping Jeannie out of the doldrums and into action. She checked the mare and, finding that she was fully dilated, moved into position to catch the foal that was about to make its entry into the world.

"Need any help?"

Alarmed, Jeannie dropped her hands and looked up.

Rafe was standing at the opening of the stall.

"You startled me." She'd been so busy concentrating on Lady she hadn't heard the barn door sliding open or his bootsteps coming down the concrete passageway.

"I didn't mean to."

"I know."

"You still haven't answered my question." Though his offer to help had been made in a friendly enough fashion, his handsome face remained remote, as if he fully expected her to refuse.

"How about some moral support instead?" She kept her voice steady, her careful tone a masquerade for her apprehension.

"You've got it." Rafe's answering smile erased the fine new lines of strain around his firm mouth.

She yawned, the emotional highs and lows of the past twenty-four hours suddenly catching up with her. "What time is it, anyway?"

He shot the cuff of his clean chambray shirt back and glanced at the old watch he wore for working the range. "A quarter after five."

"No wonder I'm so tired."

"You've been up all night."

Their gazes met over the laboring Lady's head.

I couldn't sleep, sad gray eyes said.

Me either, somber blue eyes replied.

The exchange lasted several seconds before the neighing mare reclaimed their attention.

"Come on, baby," she urged as a sac, slick and shiny and purple, bulged from under the mare's tail. "Come to Mama."

Lady gave a last mighty push and her foal slid into the world via Jeannie's outstretched hands.

Rafe joined her in the stall, kneeling beside her and blowing gently into the colt's nostrils to clear its air passages after she'd stripped away its birth sac.

"Look at that blaze on his forehead," Rafe noted.

"Just like his father."

A spasm of regret crossed Rafe's face at Jeannie's remark. Seeing it, she fell silent and sat back on her heels. When he finally spoke, he opened the floodgates for both of them.

"I should have been with you when Tony was born."

"Be glad you weren't."

"Why?"

"Because when I wasn't crying for you, I was cursing you."

"I'm surprised you still don't hate my guts."

"I love you, Rafe. I always have and I always will."

At her heartfelt declaration he drew her back up on her knees and into his arms so that they were facing each other. "I love you, too, Jeannie."

She looked at him, her eyes brimming with tears. "I wanted to cut my tongue out yesterday."

He stroked her hair, her beautiful hair. "I've been called a hell of a lot worse."

"But not by me."

"No, by myself."

Jeannie realized then that Rafe was telling her that his days of running scared were over, and she wanted to weep for joy.

The mare whickered as if to say four was a crowd, so they got to their feet and stepped out of the stall.

Rafe put his arm around Jeannie's shoulder as, still enthralled by the miracle they'd just witnessed, they watched Lady begin licking her progeny's shiny coat, massaging him with her tongue and imprinting him with her scent.

They shared a laugh when the colt, his whisk-broom of a tail rotating wildly for balance, stood for the first time on bandy legs that threatened to collapse beneath him. And they shed a tear when he finally mustered his forces and found his mother's milk.

"I'm going to tell my parents about Tony after I finish in court on Wednesday," Rafe said. "And as soon as they've recovered from the shock, I'm going to call a press conference and publicly acknowledge him as my son."

Jeannie, feeling choked up, took a deep breath. "That's wonderful, but . . ."

"But what?"

"What about your campaign?"

"I figure if I put it behind me now, the furor will have died down by next year's primary."

"That way we can concentrate on the real issues, like improving our schools and—"

"Jeannie . . ."

"What?"

"You're starting to sound like a politician's wife."

"I'm just getting warmed up."

He pulled her into his arms again. "It's going to be a tough race trying to beat an incumbent."

She smiled up at him and said simply, "Run, Rafe, run."

Outside the barn dawn replaced the indigo darkness with pewter light and suffused the Texas sky with promise. Inside, the parents of a ten-year-old boy greeted the new day with a fervent kiss and fresh commitment to winning the stubborn little turkey over.

Tony couldn't seem to get the hang of roping the calf.

Rafe, watching him make yet another overhand toss that fell short of the mark, knew what his problem was. What he didn't know was how to "show him the ropes" without putting him on the defensive . . . or himself in the painful position of being rejected again.

Shoulders slumping dejectedly, Tony reined in his gray cow pony and started recoiling—too tightly, Rafe noticed—his nylon lariat. As if to add insult to injury, the unfettered calf kicked dust in the boy's face.

"Here, take over for me." Rafe handed the branding iron he'd just heated to the cowman who was helping him. Then he headed toward the camp's picket line, where his saddled gelding was tethered along with Jeannie's mare, Rusty's bay, and several other horses.

There was more than one way to skin a cat, he mused as he mounted. Or, to put it more literally, to snare a calf. And as he took both the reins and the braided rawhide lariat he preferred to the more commonly used nylon in his left hand, he had every intention of catching two slippery critters with one toss.

Without looking back to confirm it, Rafe sensed Jeannie's smiling endorsement of the action he was taking. She'd drawn the job of vaccinating today, which meant they were working within whispering distance of each other. Even so, they'd exchanged fewer than a dozen words of a personal nature. Their lingering gazes, though, had sizzled with passionate need and pure frustration.

He chirruped to the gelding now and reined it in in a half circle, spurred by a premonition that the future of three people was riding on what he was about to do. If he could rope Tony in, if only for a few minutes, it would go a long way toward removing that last barrier between him and Jeannie.

Rafe could tell by the way Tony straightened his shoulders and sat taller in the saddle that he'd piqued his interest with the rawhide lariat. Still, he pretended not to notice that the boy was watching him work the milling calves. He simply picked out one and moved in on it.

While his gelding kept its eyes glued to the pursued animal, Rafe got ready to drop his dally. He made his preparations in slow, almost exaggerated motions so that Tony, who had kneed his own pony closer to the action, wouldn't miss a thing.

Monkey see, monkey do, Rafe thought, a surge of love welling up in him when he noticed that Tony had duplicated the hold on his nylon rope right down to his little finger. He noticed, too, the guarded look on the boy's face and knew the real test was in getting him to catch the calf.

The most common ways of roping were the head and heel catches. Since the former was easier to master than the latter, Rafe opted to go that route. Watching from the corner of his eye to be sure that Tony was following suit, he paid out the loop in his lariat and made an overhand toss.

Right on target, Rafe snared his calf. But the pride he took in his perfect aim paled in comparison to the pure joy he felt when Tony's nylon rope settled around the neck of the short-horned animal he'd singled out.

It would have been expecting too much to hear the boy *yip* with glee or yell his thanks for the roping lesson. For the man, for now, it was enough that he'd learned it.

Jeannie was standing by the supply trailer when Rafe and Tony rode up with their catches. Her champagne hair flowed past her shoulders. She'd lost her hat when she'd jumped to her feet and come running to meet the triumphant pair. Her jubilant heart glittered in her gray eyes.

"Nice going," Rusty said as he reached to take the lariats from father and son and lead the frantically lowing beasts to the branding fire.

That was when everything went wrong.

Maybe he didn't get a good enough grip on the ropes. After all, his arthritis had been bothering him terribly of late. Or maybe he tripped, further spooking the already frightened calves. No one could say for sure but Rusty. And when the cloven hooves were stilled and the dust began to settle, Rusty wasn't talking. He was lying on the ground.

For a paralyzed instant Jeannie just stood there, waiting for him to get up. The horrifying realization that he wasn't going to finally galvanized her into action. After checking to be certain that Tony and Rafe were all right, she ran to Rusty's side.

"Don't move him," she said, somehow managing to remember that that was the cardinal rule of first aid.

The two cowboys who'd been about to lift him onto a hastily unrolled sleeping bag backed off, and she knelt down beside him. Not being a medical expert, she didn't know how to ease his suffering. But seeing his torn shirt and trampled chest, looking at his blood-speckled lips and into his pain-glazed eyes, she knew that Rusty Pride had just participated in his last roundup.

"Laurrinda . . . ?" he rasped out into the shocked silence that had fallen shortly after he had.

Hot tears blurred Jeannie's vision when she realized that, in his delirium, the veteran cowhand had confused her with her mother. She patted his knobby hand consolingly, wondering how to respond. Then, knowing it was the least she could do for him after all he'd done for her, she swallowed past the lump in her throat and leaned down to whisper, "I'm here."

Rallying ever so slightly, Rusty snagged several strands of her golden hair with his gnarled fingers. The tug at her scalp was nothing compared to the tug at her heart-strings when next he spoke.

"I told you . . . your hair . . . would grow back."

Then the last cowboy let go of Jeannie's hair and joined the lady he'd worshipped from afar.

The bedroom light shone like a beacon as the woman stepped to the window and watched the taillights of the man's Studebaker disappear into the night.

Thirteen

A small greenhouse, added on at some un-known point in time to the back of Rusty's bungalow, answered the question of who had been leaving those beautiful yellow roses on Laurrinda's grave.

"I told you someone besides Grandpa might be doing it," Tony said with the slightly supe-rior air of one who'd discovered he was right.

Jeannie smoothed down his cowlick, then hugged him close, saddened to think of all the lonely years poor Rusty had wasted pining for a woman who, more for economic reasons than emotional ones, would never have left her husband had she lived.

"Phew!" Tony pinched his nostrils together and pulled a face. "It smells like a funeral parlor in here."

While she didn't agree with him, neither did Jeannie argue. She just inhaled deeply, drawing in the attar of roses and holding its sweetness inside her for a moment. Then she ushered Tony out of the greenhouse and closed the door on Rusty's monument to unrequited love.

Mother and son had walked the mile from the main house to get the suit, shirt, and tie Rusty would wear for the rest of time. They headed for his bedroom in silence, each of them lost in their own thoughts.

"Are you ready to go?" Jeannie asked a few minutes later as she folded the garments she'd taken out of the closet over her arm. When Tony didn't answer her, she turned to see what he was doing.

He was sitting on the side of Rusty's neatly made twin bed, the pocketknife that Big Tom had left him in hand. Its old ivory handle wore a yellowish cast in the morning sunlight coming through the window. And the pull of the past warred with a fear of the future on his little boy's face.

"Tony?" she prompted softly.

"I forgot to tell him thanks," he said in a small voice.

She shook her head in confusion. "Tell who thanks, honey?"

"Rafe." Uncertainly he peered up at her. "For teaching me the head catch yesterday."

"You can tell him when he comes back," she said, reaching out to stroke his cheek.

"Don't you mean *if* he comes back?" he demanded with a touch of his old defiance.

Jeannie thought she understood, at least in part, why he was blowing so hot and cold toward Rafe right now. After all, she'd been something of a basket case herself after that phone call last night.

The three of them had just finished eating dinner and started discussing plans for Rusty's funeral when Rafe's secretary called to tell him that a woman he was representing in a bitterly contested divorce had been threatened with physical harm by her husband and was in need of a restraining order to keep him out of the house. Naturally he'd said he would leave immediately for San Antonio. And since he had to be in court on another matter this morning anyway, he'd decided he would stay in town overnight and drive back to the ranch later today.

Not again! Jeannie had wanted to shout when Rafe had hung up the phone and gone to pack. She'd sat there in a complete panic for a moment, fighting all the insecurities that had rushed back with full force. Then she'd jumped up from the table and bolted after him, ready to beg him, if necessary, to let someone else go to the woman's rescue . . . ready to remind him, unfair as it sounded, that he'd said he was tired of protecting other people.

By the time she'd caught up with him at the fourplex, though, she'd calmed down enough to realize that this wasn't anything like eleven years ago, when he'd seemingly disappeared off the face of the earth. She knew where he was going and when he was coming back. And his good-bye kiss, a lusty Valentino job that left her lips throbbing and her body tingling, had told her in no uncertain terms that he'd be returning for the rest.

"He'll be back," Jeannie declared in response to Tony's doubting question.

"Okay." Still sounding unconvinced, he stood and stuck the knife in his jeans pocket. Then he picked up his blue neon cap and Rusty's best white shirt, both of which he'd set on the bed.

"Ready?"

He shook his head. "About last night . . . ?"

She nodded encouragingly. "What about it?"

"After Rafe asked you if you minded if he invited his parents to come to Rusty's funeral . . ."

"Mmm-hmm."

"And you said, 'What a good idea; I'd love to see Maria and . . .'"

Jeannie had never lied to Tony about the circumstances surrounding his birth. When he'd asked her why he didn't have a father like all the other kids, she'd just answered in the calmest voice possible that his father couldn't marry her. And when he'd pestered her for a name, she'd promised to give him one when he was older.

"Yes," she said, thinking that maybe now was the time to give him that name.

"And *who?*"

"Antonio."

Tony fidgeted and cleared his throat, as if he were getting ready to comment on the similarity between their first names.

"Anybody home?" Rafe called through Rusty's open front door.

Jeannie's mind, already jumping through the blazing hoop of truth, went into a spin at the unexpected interruption.

"We're in here!" Tony hollered, his voice wavering between "Welcome back" and "Why so early?"

Rafe, seeming to realize an explanation was in order, supplied one as he stepped into the living room and shut the door behind him. "After I got my client's restraining order last night, I called the judge on my other case at home and requested a continuance for emergency reasons."

Tony turned to greet his father, then turned back to his mother, obviously bugged by what they'd discovered in the greenhouse. "Why do you think Rusty did it?"

Jeannie heard Rafe's firm bootsteps coming toward the bedroom and smiled. "Because sometimes a person's first love is also their last."

"Where's Tony?"

"Sleeping out."

Rafe frowned. "Do you think that's a good idea."

Jeannie shrugged. "He really wanted to do it."

"What if he gets scared?"

"One of the hands will bring him home."

"How long have you known these guys?" he asked suspiciously.

She clapped her hand over his mouth.

"You know what you sound like?"

He shook his head.

"A new father."

" 'At's what I am," he mumbled against her hand.

She burst into laughter and let him go.

They were standing in the entryway, having just escorted Martha to her front door at the fourplex after helping her set the dining room table for tomorrow.

Moonlight poured down the staircase through the tall window on the landing, adding silver highlights to Jeannie's golden hair and deepening the blue of Rafe's eyes to the color of midnight. In this small, semidark world they were temporarily inhabiting, sounds and textures and smells were magnified in importance. The lilt in her voice and the smile in his, her smooth silk blouse and his rough cotton shirt, the wildflower scent of her soap and the woody essence of his after-shave . . . They were more aware of each other, more attuned to each other, than they'd ever been before.

"So," he said, sliding his arms around her waist and drawing her toward the heat of him, "our son is sleeping out and we're all alone tonight, right?"

"Right." She lifted her hands to his face and let her fingers explore a sleek eyebrow, the ridge of a cheekbone, a jaw raspy as the finest grade of sandpaper.

"Then make room for Daddy," he warned on a low growl, wedging her thighs apart with his knee at the same time that he claimed her mouth in a searing kiss.

But Daddy wasn't the only one who wanted this, and Mommy made sure he knew it. She parted her lips and answered the plunging demand of his tongue with a demand of her own.

The kiss lengthened, becoming an act of love. His tongue stroked the roof of her mouth, the pearl glaze of her teeth, the moist satin lining of her cheek. She clutched at his hair with her hands, pressed his breasts into his chest, and rubbed her body against his hard one.

When he finally lifted his mouth from hers, he buried his face in the fragrant hollow between her shoulder and neck and said in a ragged breath, "Do you realize we've made a baby but we've never made love in a bed?"

She arched her throat, pleasure flowing through her veins like warm oil and passion, adding a quiver to her voice. "There's a four-poster upstairs we could use to rectify that."

That was all the invitation he needed. He scooped her into his arms and carried her up the stairs for their first, but not their last, loving in a bed. And the light in her window, *their* window now, burned long into the night.

Seeing as how Rusty had been Laurrinda's right-hand man, that was where they buried him, to her right. And since he'd grown those yellow roses especially for her, they brought them out of the greenhouse and transplanted them in a corner of the cemetery, making a small, sweetly perfumed garden of memories.

The gathering at the gravesite wasn't as well attended as the one that had taken place ten days ago. There were a variety of reasons, one being that Rusty hadn't been as widely known as Big Tom and another being that he'd never been much of a man for fanfare.

But the important people were there: the woman who'd looked upon him as a surrogate father when she was growing up; the man who'd learned the rudiments of riding and roping from him; the boy who had a new teacher now.

And the others, no less important for being

mentioned last: the cowhands who'd ridden for the brand with him more years than they could count; the cook whom he'd called "crotchety" even as he'd gobbled up everything she'd ever set before him; the Mexican-American grandparents who'd been as anxious for a first look at their ten-year-old grandson as they'd been careful not to rush him.

Now the service was over and everyone had gone back to the main house for a bite of lunch and a bit of catching up . . . everyone except Jeannie and Rafe and Tony.

The three of them had lagged behind, speaking fondly of the man they'd just buried and skirting the monumental truth that foretold a change in their lives.

"Rusty taught me how to whittle," Tony bragged.

"Me too," Rafe said, much to the boy's surprise.

Jeannie smiled. "He made me a jewelry box when I got my ears pierced."

"Remember the time he took us waterskiing?"

"Do I ever!"

Rafe and Jeannie looked at each other and laughed.

"What's so funny?" Tony demanded, wanting in on the joke.

"Rusty tied our ski ropes around his saddle horn—"

"And let his horse pull us in place of a boat."

"I did a face-bust," Rafe reminisced wryly.

"Well, I lost my swimming-suit top," Jeannie recalled on a laugh.

Tony's assessing gaze darted from one grown-up face to the other. "You guys sure have known each other a long time, huh?"

"We sure have," the adults answered in unison.

He focused in on Rafe now. "Are you and Mom getting married?"

Rafe nodded. "I think it's about time, don't you?"

Instead of replying to what essentially was a rhetorical question, Tony pulled the knife Big Tom had left him out of his pants pocket. He looked at it for the longest moment of his parents' lives. Then he put it away and, after taking a cleansing breath, said to Rafe, "My first name is almost the same as your father's."

"And your middle name is exactly the same as Big Tom's."

"Someone at Grandpa's funeral said I looked just like you."

"The spitting image."

Jeannie, standing at the apex of this perfect triangle, held both a tremulous silence and a joyful breath.

Tony frowned. "You're my father, aren't you?"

Rafe smiled, wanting to shout it to the world. "Yes, I am."

"Well . . ." Tony went into his famous fidgeting act, then, scratching his head and his nose and shuffling from foot to foot, before he finally got up the nerve to ask the question that had been bothering him all this time. "*Where've you been?*"

Rafe was quiet for a moment, weighing the price of revenge against the priceless promise of family.

This was the opportunity he'd been waiting for, praying for, dreaming of, for eleven long years. With a few carefully chosen words he could crush Big Tom's memory and drive it out of Tony's mind. He could destroy that bigoted SOB the way he'd once tried to destroy him. Ruin him in Jeannie's eyes by repeating the horrible things the rancher had said to him that long-ago day.

But at what cost to the boy and to the woman who owned him heart and soul?

Suddenly he realized the bitterness was less strong than it used to be. Big Tom was dead, and he didn't have a damned thing left to prove to that bastard. Just as suddenly he realized he already had his revenge. The *best* revenge possible.

"I've been looking for you, son." Rafe put an arm around Tony, felt small arms hug him back as a lost child found his father. Then he reached for Jeannie with his other arm, saw the silvery sheen in her eyes as he drew her into the family circle. "I've been looking for you and your mother."

Epilogue

State Senator Rafe Martinez stepped up to the speaker's podium to take the oath for his first term in office. Beside him, wearing one of the smartly styled maternity suits that were part of her English teacher's wardrobe, stood his wife of eighteen months. And beside her squirmed their eleven-year-old son.

Rafe's voice rang out loud and clear as, with right hand raised, he swore to uphold and defend the constitutions of both the state of Texas and the United States of America, leaving no doubt in anyone's mind that he would fight to the death to protect the rights and freedoms guaranteed by those grand old documents.

The audience in the gallery overlooking the senate chambers applauded as one when the five-minute ceremony drew to an end. It had been a hard-fought campaign, pitting a good-old-boy incumbent who'd consistently broken his campaign promises against an intense dark horse who'd vowed to carry the banner for all his constituents.

Just as Jeannie had once surmised, the electorate had forgiven Rafe his youthful indiscretion. Oh, true, the media vultures had feasted on the story for months. But the voters had spoken in spite of the headlines. And in the long run that was what really counted.

Now, as the darkly handsome senator from San Antonio turned to kiss his golden-haired wife and their son, the applause resumed and rose to a standing ovation.

This man and this woman personified the new Texas—a state where people were judged on their honesty and their ability to do the job, not their heritage or their ancestors' country of origin. And this family of three, soon to be four, represented the best of two worlds.

THE EDITOR'S CORNER

Nothing could possibly put you in more of a carefree, summertime mood than the six LOVESWEPTs we have for you next month. Touching, tender, packed with emotion and wonderfully happy endings, our six upcoming romances are real treasures.

The first of these priceless stories is SARAH'S SIN by Tami Hoag, LOVESWEPT #480, a heart-grabbing tale that throbs with all the ecstasy and uncertainty of forbidden love. When hero Dr. Matt Thorne is injured, he finds himself recuperating in his sister's country inn—with a beautiful, untouched Amish woman as his nurse. Sarah Troyer's innocence and sweetness make the world seem suddenly new for this world-weary Romeo, and he woos her with his masterful bedside manner. The brash ladies' man with the bad-boy grin is Sarah's romantic fantasy come true, but there's a high price to pay for giving herself to one outside the Amish world. You'll cry and cheer for these two memorable characters as they risk everything for love. A marvelous LOVESWEPT from a very gifted author.

From our very own Iris Johansen comes a LOVESWEPT that will drive you wild with excitement—A TOUGH MAN TO TAME, #481. Hero Louis Benoit is a tiger of the financial world, and Mariana Sandell knows the danger of breaching the privacy of his lair to appear before him. Fate has sent her from Sedikhan, the glorious setting of many of Iris's previous books, to seek out Louis and make him a proposition. He's tempted, but more by the mysterious lady herself than her business offer. The secret terror in her eyes arouses his tender, protective instincts, and he vows to move heaven and earth to fend off danger . . . and keep her by his side. This grand love story will leave you breathless. Another keeper from Iris Johansen.

IN THE STILL OF THE NIGHT by Terry Lawrence, LOVESWEPT #482, proves beyond a doubt that nothing could be more romantic than a sultry southern evening. Attorney Brad Lavalier certainly finds it so, especially when he's stealing a hundred steamy kisses from Carolina Palmette. A heartbreaking scandal drove this proud beauty from her Louisiana hometown years before, and now she's back to settle her grandmother's affairs. Though she's stopped believing in the magic of love, working with devilishly sexy Brad awakens a long-denied hunger within her. And only he can slay the dragons of her past and melt her resistance to a searing attraction. Sizzling passion and deep emotion—an unbeatable combination for a marvelous read from Terry Lawrence.

Summer heat is warming you now, but your temperature will rise even higher with ever-popular Fayrene Preston's newest LOVESWEPT, FIRE WITHIN FIRE, #483. Meet powerful businessman Damien Averone, brooding, enigmatic—and burning with need for Ginnie Summers. This alluring woman bewitched him from the moment he saw her on the beach at sunrise, then stoked the flame of his desire with the entrancing music of her guitar on moonlit nights. Only sensual surrender will soothe his fiery ache for the elusive siren. But Ginnie knows the expectations that come with deep attachment, and Damien's demanding intensity is overwhelming. Together these tempestuous lovers create an inferno of passion that will sweep you away. Make sure you have a cool drink handy when you read this one because it is hot, hot, hot!

Please give a big and rousing welcome to brand-new author Cindy Gerard and her first LOVESWEPT—MAVERICK, #484, an explosive novel that will give you a charge. Hero Jesse Kincannon is one dynamite package of rugged masculinity, sex appeal, and renegade ways you can't resist. When he returns to the Flying K Ranch and fixes his smoldering gaze on Amanda Carter, he makes her his own, just as he did years before when she'd been the foreman's young daughter and he was the boss's son. Amanda owns half the ranch now, and Jesse's sudden reappearance is suspicious. However, his outlaw kisses soon convince her that he's after her heart. A riveting romance from one of our New Faces of '91! Don't miss this fabulous new author!

Guaranteed to brighten your day is SHARING SUNRISE by Judy Gill, LOVESWEPT #485. This utterly delightful story features a heroine who's determined to settle down with the only man she has ever wanted . . . except the dashing, virile object of her affection doesn't believe her love has staying power. Marian Crane can't deny that as a youth she was filled with wanderlust, but Rolph McKenzie must realize that now she's ready to commit herself for keeps. This handsome hunk is wary, but he gives her a job as his assistant at the marina—and soon discovers the delicious thrill of her womanly charms. Dare he believe that her eyes glitter not with excitement over faraway places but with promise of forever? You'll relish this delectable treat from Judy Gill.

And be sure to look for our FANFARE novels next month—three thrilling historicals with vastly different settings and times. Ask your bookseller for A LASTING FIRE by the bestselling author of THE MORGAN WOMEN, Beverly Byrne, IN THE SHADOW OF THE MOUNTAIN by the beloved Rosanne Bittner, and THE BONNIE BLUE by LOVESWEPT's own Joan Elliott Pickart.

Happy reading!

With every good wish,

Carolyn Nichols

Carolyn Nichols
Publisher, FANFARE and LOVESWEPT

60 Minutes to a Better, More Beautiful You!

Now it's easier than ever to awaken your sensuality, stay slim forever—even make yourself irresistible. With Bantam's bestselling subliminal audio tapes, you're only 60 minutes away from a better, more beautiful you!

__ 45004-2	**Slim Forever**	$8.95
__ 45035-2	**Stop Smoking Forever**	$8.95
__ 45022-0	**Positively Change Your Life** ...	$8.95
__ 45041-7	**Stress Free Forever**	$8.95
__ 45106-5	**Get a Good Night's Sleep**	$7.95
__ 45094-8	**Improve Your Concentration** .	$7.95
__ 45172-3	**Develop A Perfect Memory**	$8.95

Bantam Books, Dept. LT, 414 East Golf Road, Des Plaines, IL 60016

Please send me the items I have checked above. I am enclosing $_____ (please add $2.50 to cover postage and handling). Send check or money order, no cash or C.O.D.s please. (Tape offer good in USA only.)

Mr/Ms _____

Address _____

City/State _____ Zip _____

LT-2/91

Please allow four to six weeks for delivery.
Prices and availability subject to change without notice.